Alan ... 922.
He le... his
father's farm, spending his spare time sailing on the
Norfolk Broads and writing nature notes for the *Eastern*
... *s*. He also wrote poetry, some of which was
... while he was in the RAF during the Second
... r. By 1950, he was running his own bookshop
... ich. In 1955, the first of what would become a
... f forty-six George Gently novels was published.
... d in 2005, aged eighty-two.

The Inspector George Gently series

Gently Continental

Alan Hunter

ROBINSON

Constable & Robinson Ltd
55–56 Russell Square
London WC1B 4HP
www.constablerobinson.com

First published in the UK by Cassell & Company Ltd, 1967

This paperback edition published by Robinson,
an imprint of Constable & Robinson Ltd, 2012

A copy of the British Library Cataloguing in
Publication Data is available from the British Library

ISBN: 978-1-78033-942-9 (paperback)
ISBN: 978-1-78033-943-6 (ebook)

Typeset by TW Typesetting, Plymouth, Devon

Printed and bound in the UK

1 3 5 7 9 10 8 6 4 2

CHAPTER ONE

WHAT IS MAKE-BELIEVE? Is it any more than a label for an attitude?

Consider, for example, this Hotel Continental of Mrs Breske's, from which, even when you're on the beach, you can hear strains of accordion and zither – on an English beach, please note, combed by the British Territorial North Sea, with a few miles south, jutting out spiderily, the pale iron-work of an English resort pier, where there will be Bingo Tonite and every Nite, throughout the season, and imitation food is being served in imitation restaurants – this hotel, formerly the Grand, lying in a hollow between crumbling brown cliffs, facing east towards Holland and lanes of distant busy ships, English in every red brick, every slate, every sash window, backed by English fields, an English village and the solid unreason of English roads: English, if ever a thing were English, in its apparent sins and virtues, drearily, wearily English, unlikely to be claimed by any other nation; yet in which, Herr Brown, Herr Robinson, Herr Smith, Herr Jones, if you step, you step into a –

slightly pre-war – Viennese establishment, with an alpenhorn for tourists to remark on gleaming extensively above the reception-booth, and a smell of floor-polish delicately tempered by a smell of most un-English pastry.

Make-believe?

But isn't Mrs Breske an *echte Tochter* of Vienna, born, not like her mother, in Leopoldstadt, but on the right side of the Radetsky Bridge? Second daughter of old Max Tichtel, twenty years chef at Romanoff's, who (poor old man, it is his only pleasure) she visits each year, during the off-season? Yes, yes, and herself a cook, celebrated for strudel pastry, a favourite pupil of Willi Schmidt's (the great Willi, of whom you have heard), doing very well until she married that scapegrace fiddler, Martin Breske, who left her with two children, one a baby, and of whom the less said the better. Oh yes, she is Viennese! Though now she has lived in England so long. Perhaps because she has lived there so long. Her English grows worse every year.

Make-believe?

Listen again to the plunking twangle of the zither, the mechanical fluting of the accordion, the rippling laughter of young Trudi Breske – Trudi, so flamboyantly Austrian, china eyes, flaxen hair, always laughing at what men say to her, and they say a great deal – look about you at the eager young waiters, the maids dressed in operetta costumes, the dark, tall-stemmed bottles, beer steins, menus and wine-lists printed in German. What is make-believe? To pretend? But what is Mrs Breske pretending? She creates her Hotel Continental in her own image, and it is what it is. The world she was torn from in 1937 continued with her, because it was her. To her, make-believe was war-time London, deprivation, bombs, foreigners. The real, Vienna, continued eternally in the outward shape of her thickening figure, sprang forth in words, gestures, tears, some little things on the dressing-table. And then, when times changed, when the war was over, when the Nazis left, when the local Gauleiters, who included her uncle, were put behind bars and stripped of their loot, when she went back to Vienna to claim the estate of her dead sister, rightfully hers: lo, there stood a Vienna other than the Vienna of Mrs Breske. What could she do, poor woman, finding herself so denied? Except in her, Vienna had vanished: she was less of a foreigner in London. She found old friends, and cried with them, but it was an effort rather than a relief. Her very daughters spoke German so execrably that they were cheated by shopkeepers, who took them for tourists. Oh, oh, she would never forget her first return visit to Vienna. As soon as she could she collected her money, and cried all the way back to London.

Make-believe? Is it any more than a label for an attitude? A pejorative term used when we are reminded that our own reality is purely relative?

So Mrs Breske, middle-aged, a cook, a Viennese cook, with money left her by her sister, buys an old sea-side hotel, calls it the Hotel Continental, ransacks the Vienna of her dreams, creates about herself the outward image of the cosmos of Edith Breske: not Vienna as it was or is but a Breskeian extension, real, as fire burns is real, false, but no falser, than the beholder's eye. And it pays, pretty well, since Mrs Breske is business, and her daughter, Frieda, she's business, while Trudi is excellent decoration. Trudi will probably marry. Frieda probably won't marry. Trudi is the darling of the guests. Frieda makes out their bills. Trudi is gay, is innocent – it may be too innocent. Frieda is dark and grey-eyed, far from gay, perhaps not so innocent. Mrs Breske, nearing fifty, is not innocent at all. Her husband-less life has always been solaced by regular and mindless love-making. Frieda notices, but says nothing. Trudi apparently doesn't notice. At the moment the newest of the four waiters, Carlo, is taking up Mrs Breske's night cap. Carlo. Carlo Gordini. A dark-eyed waiter from Milan.

Make-believe? A woman with a man has surely some right to be regarded as real?

Listen again to that music. This is a particular night in July. A warm night. Even the sea breeze has died right away. Dinner is over – oh, a perfect dinner, lying lightly on the stomach – and some of the guests are sitting on the lawn, watching the sparkling flash of the lightship. And just below them the English sea is lying almost asleep, and an English tide is very softly washing along an English beach. Zither, accordion and fiddle. Something of Strauss's? Perhaps not. Cafe music. That strain again. Does it matter what it's called? Time to retire, but the night so perfect, the stars dusted on a gun-blue sky, the liquid air, the smell of the sea, the smoky yellow lamp of a longshore boat. Who could paint it, suddenly so moving, of a thousand nights, one? Mrs Breske has long since retired, Carlo has taken up her hot milk and brandy. Trudi, who was playing tennis with the guests all day, sleeps dreamlessly, her windows wide, only a sheet pulled

4

over her. Frieda alone, grey-eyed Frieda, yet sits sulkily at the desk, waiting for the key-board to empty, waiting to lock up the doors. Pause, please. Look at Frieda. Twenty-nine-year-old Frieda. Frieda who takes after her mother. Pale. Rounded cheek-bones. Ovoid chin. Rather square in the shoulder, rather long in the body, moves with the air of it being an effort, but heavy-boned, strong. Frieda hunched over a paperback, turning pages rapidly, careless if she's looked at because men rarely look at her twice. Sulky. A thinking woman. Yes, look at Frieda. But now the musicians, who have a rostrum in the dining-room, are yawning and putting away their instruments, are going off to the kitchen for coffee and a sandwich. Frieda frowns, glances towards them, glances at the clock, the huge carved wood clock, glances through the foyer to the lawn: and sure enough, the guests are rising from their chairs. A lovely evening, Miss Breske. Thank you, Frieda . . . a lovely evening. An early call, please. Thank you. Did the American come in? – did he? Frieda glances at the key-board and looks sour. He didn't. Earlier, she'd seen him go out herself, that ugly, quiet, untypical American. The American who didn't take photographs, make calls, receive letters, but who talked in a thick Bronx accent and wore sky-blue shirts with silver stars on them. The American. Their American – because he had adopted the Hotel Continental. He guessed it suited him, was real restful, maybe he'd stop over a few weeks. So becoming their American. Wilbur Clooney, their American. Whom Frieda despised, and let it show, and who now would have to ring the bell to get in. To make certain, she locks the swing doors first of all, latches windows (the American has the cheek of the devil), then proceeds to the kitchen quarters, there to make her fortress secure. So the American will have to ring. And she herself will refuse to hear him. Miss Breske, Frieda, on a lovely night in July. And they retire, the guests, the musicians, the waiters, the maids in black bodices, the assistant chefs, the kitchen boy, and lastly Frieda, Miss Breske. Taking a last look from her bedroom window, at her mother's window across the courtyard. But her mother's window is dark. And no American is ringing the bell. So, so, the night hours pass over the Hotel Continental, which houses who knows what slumber, what dreams, what fornications, what ease and unease, till, at first just a hardening of the horizon, far out to sea, beyond the lightship, then a paling and yellowing many leagues off, as though there lay now a country unperceived by day, then a pallor feeling up the sky, developing perspective, beginning shadows, dawn stretches up from the eastward and the longshore boatmen dowse their glim. Still do they sleep in the Hotel Continental, while the trumpets of the morning are sounding? While the silly larks rise and trill over the marrams, while the blackbirds are bursting their throats? All still, nobody stirring? But there's the bell, and there again: and again, and again, somebody ringing, ringing, ringing. Up somebody – answer the door! Frieda, pull on your old dressing-gown. Mrs Breske, are you deaf – don't you hear that bell tolling? But who can be ringing at half-past four, ringing, ringing, ringing, ringing? The locks, the bolts, dawn breaks down the door. A man's voice, mumbling. A shriek – that's the maid. Mrs Breske's voice, querulous, mixing German with English. The man's voice again. Frieda, stealing along the landing. What's the matter? Who knows? It's one of the fishermen, wearing great leather thigh-boots. You can't understand what he says, or what Mrs Breske says either, and the maid has fainted, or is pretending to faint, down there on the bench carved like an eagle. And now Frieda is there, asking quick questions, Frieda in a sagging blue dressing-gown, giving orders, slapping the maid, riding over her mother's emotional pother. Get back to bed – I'll see to it. That's what Frieda is telling Mrs Breske. Ja, ja, but – Get back to bed. Ach, mein Gott, Frieda – Leave it to me. And suddenly Mrs Breske is howling, is shedding tears like a cloudburst – mein Gott, mein Gott – ach, Frieda, Frieda! But she does what Frieda says, she comes bellowing up the stairs, and the guests crowded on the landing dare not ask what the matter is. How she roars, this Mrs Breske, how she rocks as she stumbles along, how she cries first into her two hands this side, then into her two hands that side. And when she has stumbled into her room, which is some way distant from the guest rooms, still she roars, though someone is comforting her, someone, not she, slams the door. Meanwhile the fisherman stands below in his thigh-boots, his tan jumper, a huge man with a red face and hands hanging open at his sides, a great child of a man, looking foolish and embarrassed, waiting, eyes lowered, not moving an inch. For what is he waiting? Ah, back comes Frieda. She has fetched two waiters from the kitchen annex. Some low words – too low to catch, but the two shake their tousled heads – then the waiters and the fisherman go out together, and behind them Frieda bolts the doors. What can possibly have happened? From Mrs Breske's room, subdued moanings. In the hall, Frieda standing alone, Frieda, Miss Breske, in her blue dressing-gown. And the sun rises. And the sea sharpens. And the blackbirds, though not the larks, tire. And it is almost again as though nothing had happened, or nothing in particular, at the Hotel Continental.

Make-believe? But no! Something indeed has happened, something in terms of experience, or reality, shouldering mental worlds aside: something shocking, as people call it, when their system of concepts is paralysed, when, against their will, their consciousness is modified, and their identity suddenly at question. Something shocking – but what, and to whom? Somebody thinks of the American. Yes, the American. He didn't come in. He certainly went out, but didn't come in. Could it, was it . . . did he go swimming? Obviously the fishermen had found him. And that innocent sea by that innocent beach had a treacherous current on the ebb, had drowned strong swimmers, was the subject of a stricture by the local coroner. But wasn't it an unusual time to go swimming, especially after a Breskeian dinner – to which, as those who sat nearest to him recall, the American did a noisy justice? He would need to be mad to go swimming after that: even though American, he'd need to be mad; and however, he'd taken no towel or costume, simply set off as for a stroll. And yes: he did the same every evening. Now people remember his evening stroll. After dinner, after his whiskies, in the cool of the twilight, he went strolling. Perhaps to meet somebody? A woman? But he

8

was never gone for long. And other guests have met him out there, on the beach, the cliffs, always alone. In fact, the American is mostly alone, it is one of his un-American traits. A lonely American, with no conversation. A mystery man. Why is he here?

And while they talk, a low chatter, Frieda is sitting at the desk, huddled, her broad chin on her hands, her grey eyes staring empty: Frieda, Miss Breske, who locked the doors against the American, who despised the American, she sits there, thinking. So like her mother, so unlike her. In features like, unlike in character. No tears from Miss Breske, no hysteria, no volubility, no tags of German left over from her Vienna childhood; a drab, sad girl, a business girl, a thinker. Now she picks up the phone. Who is she ringing – the police? Very composedly she speaks into it, answers questions, gives information. Yes, Miss Breske runs that hotel, notwithstanding her mother's fine cooking, her mother's Viennese fancy: she is the salt in the dish. She lays the phone down, rises. The guests on the landing fall silent. She looks up at them – quite expressionless – and several make a motion of drawing back. Are they suddenly feeling ashamed, like a group of gapers at an accident? Standing solitary in the hall Miss Breske looks so pale, so forlorn.

The bell rings again! Miss Breske hurries to the door. One of the guests, who has a sea-facing room, slips into it to stare from his window. Quick, quick! Others join him. Down there, look, covered with sacks, lying on a stretcher of a boat's floor-boards, dead for a ducat, dead he must be. Dead, dead, dead, dead. And covered with sacks on a boat's floor-boards. Drowned dead, found dead, but dead all ways. Now they carry him round the back and there's a rush to fresh windows. In there, in there, Miss Breske is saying, pointing to the timber, thatch-roofed summerhouse. She has a key, she always has keys, she opens the door, stands aside. They carry him in. The dead American. Into the summerhouse. Under his sacks. Do this, do that, her lips are saying, put him on the bench, oh, and cover him up. And this they have done, the fishermen, the waiters, because they bring out the floor-boards but not the sacks; and Miss Breske locks up, like a careful housekeeper, locks up the lonely American, dead. What happens now, says the big fisherman. Nothing, she says, I've informed the police. Just give me your names. They give her their names. They pick up the floor-boards, go humping away. And Miss Breske, and key, and the two waiters, come back from the summerhouse and into the hall. Yet – surely! – there's more to it, this dying, this tragedy? More than four old sacks and boards freckled with dried fish scales? More awe, more sentiment, more sacredness, more . . . make-believe? Or do all Americans, and perhaps other men, go dying like this?

Perhaps, even dying is a label given to an attitude.

CHAPTER TWO

Bᴜᴛ ᴏꜰ ᴄᴏᴜʀsᴇ there is more to it, the death of the Hotel Continental's American, if not at a universal, then certainly at a particular, level. Though at first he lies more quiet than ever beneath his sacks in the summer-house, attracting no notice, as he silently cools, except that of an early-flying bluebottle. But the living have formulas for the dead, however, wherever, the dying is done, and the appropriate formula, selected tentatively, is already in motion for the American: he waits, but does not wait long, under his second-hand hessian. First, from the village, comes Police Constable Stody, who in fact is a brother of the big fisherman, also a big man, a compassionate man, one who is troubled by duties of this kind; he has a few words, official and unofficial, with Mrs and Miss Breske, then reluctantly takes the key and goes to his statutory appointment with the deceased. He is brief. He removes the sacks, gazes unwillingly at what is beneath them. He notices the American's head is twisted to the left, that the skull is gory and undoubtedly fractured. Runnels of blood have dried on the face,

11

which has the mouth open, as though screaming, while the eyeballs, though caked with sand and mere carrion, express horror. Stody closes his eyes a moment, then he bends over the American. The American had been wearing a pea-green silk shirt, green hopsack trousers, a cream tussore jacket. Stody empties the pockets of trousers and jackets. They do not contain anything remarkable. He looks at the passport, which tells him the deceased was Wilbur O'Brien Clooney, of East 115A Street, New York. Stody looks for letters. There are no letters. Other than the passport, there are no documents. The passport tells him Clooney is single, is a dealer in real estate, is fifty-one. Well, his Embassy will sort that out, whether he has a next-of-kin, a mother, brother, sister Clooney who, for some reason, writes him no letters. None of Stody's business, thank Heaven. Stody has finished in the summerhouse. He recovers the body, packs the belongings in a grip, gets to hell out of there, may he never see that body again. He goes up to Clooney's room, Number 7, along with Frieda Breske, who brings the key. Number 7 is a small single at the end of the landing. In the chest, a lot of shirts, string underwear, brilliant ties. In the wardrobe, one suit and a collection of pants and jackets. Shoes, he'd a taste for English brogues, but liked them pointed and particoloured. Two suitcases with Pan-American stickers. A Mickey Spillane. That was the lot. Did he never have any mail? No letters came for Mr Clooney. Did he talk about himself, his family? Frieda Breske shakes her head. Did he deposit anything in the safe. Frieda thinks, says no.

An odd fellow, this American! What sort of picture can

Stody be forming? Probably a confused, quite uncritical picture, because, after all, there's no accounting for Americans. Didn't they take these long vacations, spending months at a time in Europe – in England, even, let alone Europe – and so perhaps here, in the Hotel Continental? An American businessman having a break, getting away from it all, letting his mail, if any, pile up elsewhere until he was good and ready to deal with it. Yes, that would be Stody's picture of the lonely American, if Stody felt a need (as perhaps yet he did not) to form a picture at all. Clooney's merely being American would blunt Stody's normal speculation. Also, occupying the foreground in his mind, was the pity he felt for the poor devil. Keep his room locked, he says, we'll fetch the stuff away later. How about – , Miss Breske says. We'll fetch him after the doctor's seen him, Stody says. And taking his grip, and thinking no evil, but still sick inside, Stody climbs into his '59 Morris Minor and drives away to his brother's house.

Fred Stody, Brother Fred, changed now out of his thigh-boots, shakes his head with Brother Jim and gives him his theory of the tragedy. It was this pill-box, he says, that's what busted his skull in, the one that toppled off the cliff. We found him lying nearly touching it. You mean he fell off the cliff on it, Stody says, and Brother Fred says, Blast, what else? Brother Fred is drinking tea laced with whisky, a cup of which he offers Stody. Anywhere else, Brother Fred says, well, he might have broke his neck. But those cliffs aren't high nor yet steep, and there's only sand at the foot of them. Blast, I once took a tumble down there, and never let on to Ma about it – I was a bit stiff for a day or two – you remember, Jim? I never broke nothing. Brother Fred sucks down some tea. It was just his bloody bad luck, he says. Anywhere else and he'd have walked away, but he had to hit that bugger head-on. Ah, you can see the spot, says Balls, skinny Sid Balls, Brother Fred's mate, blood shot out there a-rummun, like you'd hulled down a ripe tomato. Yes, that's a fact, Brother Fred says, that's a bloody fact, Jim, that is. I suppose you didn't see anything, Stody says, not at the time, when you were out there? Brother Fred scorns this suggestion, for weren't they fishing half a mile out? And between the moons, what's more, with a bit of shore-mist coming up later, laying and hauling their long, circling net from the rolling boat with its one hurricane lamp. Oh, they could see the shape of the cliffs (like the shape of their own faces they knew them, so that just by glancing at the shore, as they frequently did, they could fix their position with marvellous accuracy), and they could see the lights of the town, farther along, even the garlanded ribbons of the 'illuminations', and, before the last one went out, some while before midnight, the lights of the Hotel Continental. But see something happening on the cliffs? Brother Jim knew better than that. Nor they didn't hear a cry? Stody persists. No, nor they wouldn't and couldn't have heard a cry. Not though that mouth, death-arrested in the act, had split in twain to give the utterance passage. The linear sea, rolling in to the shore, would have captured that cry in its corrugations, may have echoed it down to surprised mermaids, but not to the fishermen lugging their nets. No, Brother Jim, it's no use pressing them, they have no titbits for the coroner, they cannot illumine

14

that dark moment when the lonely American cried, Truth. So drink Mrs Brother Fred's tea with its shot of Highland Cream.

But the ranged cliffs themselves, may they not bear witness? Those soft-lined, honey-coloured cliffs, seventy or eighty feet at their highest? Descending, scramblably, with little pockets of wiry grass and ling, at no precipitous angle, to the fawn sand of the beach? To them, still before breakfast, go the two brothers and Sid Balls, bumping and swerving along a stony track in the shiny black 1000. The track, much used by Brother Fred, winds over the hump of a hill, gives a fine view of the heathy cliff-tops, then settles again towards the beach. Stody parks just short of the beach, just short of Brother Fred's boat. They climb out. There you are then, says Brother Fred, the showman. He points up the beach. A few yards from the cliff-base is lying a grotesque concrete iceberg, three parts submerged in soft sand, one part digging at the sky. The concrete is crumbling but defiant, unlike the resigned rock of the cliffs, and from its defiance, resembling hooked fingers, stretch bent rods of rusted steel. I heard it come down, says Brother Fred, blast, I thought it was a bomb. That gale we had two years ago. I was down here seeing to the old girl. And they stand by the car for a moment contemplating this Ozymandian symbol, the pill-box which had stood on the cliff's brow, which now was buried in the lone, level sands. And that's where we saw him, Brother Fred says, when we were unloading the nets. 'Is that a bloke up there?' Sid says, and I saw him between the cliff and the pill-box. Ah, Sid Balls says, I knew he was a dead 'un, the funny way he was lying. You could see straight away, Brother Fred says, he'd come down the cliff. From the way he laid. He leads on, still the showman, along a line which previous feet have trampled, up to the pill-box, Ozymandian symbol, the precise and reverberating spot. See here, and see here. Stody, poker-faced, sees. The bloody blot with its shooting radii, as yet not quite dried. The bloody sand, kneaded, trampled. The marks where the floor-boards had lain. He sees, stares vulnerably, makes a motion with his hand. Fetch some water, he says, wash that lot off, help me kick some sand over this mess. So they fetch sea-water in a dipper and scrub and scrub the spot clean, the damned spot, they have it clean, and the bloody sand is dispersed. All under a morning sun which has some spite in it already. Now we'll look up on the cliff, Stody says, and this time Stody leads the way. They climb, perspiring lightly, up a zig-zag path, to the heathery furzy fragrant tops. Here the linnet sings, the goldfinch, flies the red-winged Cinnabar moth, lurks, to be seen suddenly after much not-seeing, and always inaccessible, the bottle-tit's nest. But these are things of no witness. They are not in Stody's eye. He looks abroad and sees – yes! directly – a green straw hat with a broad brim. The American's hat, almost certainly, for the colour is a match with his shirt: and it lies, as though carelessly thrown there, in a furze bush, fifty yards from the cliff edge. They hasten to it. Stody picks it up. It is cold with the dew just going off it. A flamboyant, flaring Italian straw, made limp by exposure. An Italian straw hat. So they look at it, and Brother Fred says, Blast, but what's it doing over here? – and they look from the hat across to the cliff-edge, and from the cliff edge back to the hat. Do you reckon something frightened him? Sid Balls says, with the sudden urgency of a shallow mind. What could've frightened him? Brother Fred says, don't talk daft, Sid, there's nothing up here. But he looks around, all the same, and so do Stody and Sid Balls. A bull? A ghost? Old Shuck the phantom – hound of staring eyes, who pads the coast roads? Did one or another of them startle the American, send him leaping, screaming over the cliff? I reckon, Brother Fred says, reaching for firmer ground, I reckon he got himself lost up here. There wasn't any moon, don't you forget it. You can easy get lost amongst these old furze bushes. But he'd know where the cliff was, Sid Balls says, he'd hear the sea if he couldn't see it. If you get panicked enough, Brother Fred says, you'll just dash around, sea or no sea. But somehow even this doesn't seem to explain the matter, though it was worth hearing how it sounded, worth putting it up in defence of reason before succumbing to the mystery of the American's hat. What do you reckon? Brother Fred asks Stody. Stody only shakes his head. He doesn't know, admits he doesn't know, supposes that now, nobody ever will. The American, that achingly unknown quantity, unanswerable for any of his peculiarities, leaves his hat some distance from the cliff-edge, here endeth a fact, place a period. I wonder if – Stody says. He moves across to the cliff-edge. There indeed, directly below him, lies the amorphous nugget of steel and concrete. He didn't just slip, says Brother Fred, coming up, if he'd just slipped he'd have missed it. He walked off, or ran off, or jumped off, but anyway he didn't just slip. They pause to consider this proposition of a walking, running or jumping American. Sid Balls says, Perhaps he thought he could fly, but Brother Fred squashes him as usual. And so, another fact, another mystery – the American didn't slip, apparent and contained in the simple geometry of cliff, beach and concrete. He removed his hat, took a running jump: no other construction is available. With the dark, dark night pressing around him he performed this inexplicable act. He must have done it on purpose, Sid Balls says, and this once Brother Fred forbears to squash him. How is it possible to resist this simple, immaculate, solution? Answering, in Stody's case, every question raised by this lonely and untypical man, offering a consummate picture of him, according to information received? Ah, that's it, Brother Fred says, either that or he was balmy. It stands to reason, Sid Balls says, swelling with vanity at his own acuteness. But if it was dark – Stody says, and they watch him, catching at his words. If it was dark, he was going to say, how had the American judged his fall so well? He doesn't say it, looks instead for any marks at the cliff-edge, but the ground hard, sour and ling-covered, is proof against chance impressions. He has been, has seen – as much as a constable needs to see on these occasions. Enough for a coroner to moralize over, devise a verdict upon, sign, dismiss. Right, Stody says, meaning right by the rules, the customs, the formula, and with the Italian straw hat in his hand he draws off to his Morris 1000.

Right thus far at all events, and much mystery understood: but another man has visited the American while Stody is taking the air of the cliff-top. He is a man with sharp tools and a sharp mind and a disciplined stomach and a good degree and more experience of police-work than he needs or in fact has time for: by name, John Halliday, F.R.C.P.(Ed.), general practitioner in that district. Halliday is waiting by the Police House when Stody returns from the cliffs. He is outside his car, leaning against it, smoking his pipe with slow puffs. A neat man, with a face that looks as though the skin is too tight for it, showing the structure of the bones; and quick, hypnotic, brown eyes. He comes round to Stody's car. Hallo, Jim, he says. Good morning, sir, Stody says, climbing, helmetless, out of the Morris. Jim, Halliday says, I've seen the body, and in a way I wish I hadn't. A nasty sight, sir, Stody says. I wish I hadn't seen it either. Jim, Halliday says. Stody waits. Halliday smokes. Jim, Halliday says, he dropped off the cliff, did he – you'll have been up there, taken a look? Just this moment, sir, Stody says, I was up there with Brother Fred. Have you any ideas, Jim? Halliday says. Well, sir, Stody says, it might have been either way. I'd say most likely it was intentional, but it could have been an accident. There's not much to go on. What was on the body? Halliday asks. Stody lifts out the grip, shows Halliday what's in it. Halliday picks up a tiny penknife, opens it, closes it, drops it back. He says, Have you found anything on the cliff? Only this hat, Stody says, exhibiting it. Nothing else? Some signs perhaps? Stody shakes his head, no, nothing. Halliday smokes for some while, then: Well, Jim, he says, well. The deceased died from head injuries and a broken neck, one or both. The deceased has bruises on the chest and also on the jaw and both wrists, and the deceased has a group of twenty-two shallow incisions, made shortly before death, in the abdomen. That's the substance of the matter, Jim, leaving out a few minor abrasions. His brown eyes flick at Stody. Stody, without his helmet, stares. Incisions, sir? Cuts, Jim. Twenty-two. Through his shirt. You mean, like stabs, sir? No, not stabs, incisions, not more than half an inch deep. Stody wrestles with this idea. Halliday smokes a little faster. Still, the image of an inscrutable American is present in a corner of Stody's mind. Could they have been – self-inflicted, sir? Halliday shrugs. Quite easily. With that – penknife? Not very likely. No signs of the blade being used lately. But they could have been. . . Then suddenly it strikes Stody, as though a sea-mist is lifted, leaving naked, no longer inscrutable, no longer essentially American, the dead man: exposing him, for the first time in Stody's mind, to the full exercise of professional logic, as though it were anyone, says Brother Fred, lying beneath the sacks in the thatched summer-house. You're thinking, sir – ? Halliday shakes his head. I'm doing no thinking for anyone, Jim. But the bruises – Are where I said they were, don't come to me for interpretations. But there were other signs, sir? He'd been down on his back. There were bents and bits of ling stuck to his jacket. Did you examine his nails, sir? He used to bite them, nothing useful there. His knuckles? Abraded in the fall. That's the lot, Jim. I'm off to breakfast. And he gets in his car, Doctor Halliday, having thrown his bomb at poor Stody, in his this-year's Rover, brightly gleaming, which glides away towards the village. Oh Stody, Jim Stody, now what panic's in thy breastie? With the coroner's court fading, changing, into an assize of cross-question? Constable Stody, did you efface, or cause to be effaced, certain bloodstains? Will you, Constable Stody, explain to the court why you saw fit to erase the footprints? Did you remove this hat from the place where you found it? What was your object, Constable Stody? In your opinion, is it not a fact, can you suggest any alternative? These dark thoughts, in simultaneous passage, hold Stody watching the departing Rover, keep him standing some moments longer, the grip, the hat in his hands.

CHAPTER THREE

B UT IF THE formula is dead, long live the formula – it is but substituting a different process for one tried and found inadequate. Or rather, it is expanding the first, simple figure, composed of Stody, Halliday and the coroner, into a more complex structure, an inverted pyramid, of which Stody is the base. To be reared how high, how wide? Till its shadow covers the dead American: when it will certainly be overspreading the Hotel Continental, the Breskes, their staff and forty-four guests. For if the American did die by another, and not decently alone, then his pyramid, financed by the tax-payers, will amaze the appetite of pharaohs. Not Cheops, in all his glory, will die as famously as Wilbur Clooney. Stody, first block in that pyramid, and already feeling himself overlaid, sits down in the office in the Police House and puts through a call to H.Q. The call is received and considered. It merits the attention of C.I.D. It relieves a Detective Inspector, Herbert Shelton, from the routine boredom of a breaking-and-entering. Then, shifting smartly up the pyramid, H.Q. inform London, and London inform Grosvenor Square, who request the documents of their dead national. Construction lines rising everywhere! Messages chase back and forth. Clooney's passport, his single document, departs for London by special messenger. Then a grape-vine, no matter whose, catches a passing echo, no matter which, and alongside the first pyramid rises, in an instant, a second and complementary structure. Headlines flame in the lunchtime editions: Ritual Slaying of American Tourist? Gashed American Found Dead. Dead American – Witchcraft Victim? And the Street hums, for news is slack, and those twenty-two incisions are pennies from heaven. Before Herbert Shelton, not as yet aware of the spotlights training on him, can do more than initiate a preliminary discussion with the Breskes and their staff; cars are beginning to scorch the gravel, the bell of the reception desk rings frantically, and a clutch of determined pressmen, cameras poised, are desiring, requiring and insisting on statements. Shelton, much photographed, is dumb. This thing has not before happened to him. In great alarm he backs into the office, slams the door, rings H.Q. It'll be the Yard for this one, says the oldest press-man, who has seen more homicides than hot dinners, and in a moment they know, are sure, are certain, and begin furbishing Yard To Be Called? paragraphs. If no news happens, go out and make some.

News, however, is making itself, beneath the eagle in Grosvenor Square, where a young attaché, Cyrus Fleischer, has been passed the lonely American's one document. Fleischer is not much interested in the document. Fleischer has lately dated a blonde. All day Cy

Fleischer has been in a daydream about this blonde, whose name is Elizabeth. He has seen Elizabeth on a series of documents, in the conference room, in the restaurant, a couple of times in the toilet, and now on the buff pages of the one document. But oddly, while staring at the one document, he finds other images disturbing Elizabeth's, like a swinging ball that knocks down buildings, bulldozers, trucks, sweating negroes. Then other images still, like himself when young (not long ago), and a girl called Cecile, Cecile Legrande, who sure as hell had no connection with Elizabeth. But there he goes, through the dust and debris, a callow kid on his first date, Cecile Legrande, a tenement girl; Pop would have tanned his hide if he'd known. But why think of that? What brought it up? Cy wrinkles his still-freckled nose. Elizabeth fades, he sees the one document, calls up a moment of official attention. Then – wow! The ball, the bulldozers, the negroes, the trucks, Cecile Legrande, they whirl again in a startled picture, and Cy whoops, This goddam passport's phoney! Because there isn't any East 115A Street, and he, Cy Fleischer, knows there isn't. Didn't he hang around, watching them knock it down, when he was running after the girl out of the tenements? Yes sir, it was flattened, wiped out, razed, in the re-zoning project in '57, became a garden-greenbelt precinct, has never been East 115A Street since. And this goddam passport – look at the date! Stamped January 5 of this year, address 78 East 115A Street, which came down before Cy went to college. Whadya know about that? The goddam passport *must* be phoney. Under no conceivable set of circumstances or procedure can it be anything else but phoney. And it is phoney – oh yes! Security tears it to small shreds. A nice fake, very nice, but look at that paper, ink, stamp. Good work, Cy, you'll make the grade, boy. Cy Fleischer. Sweating on a blonde.

And the American who had that one document, which turns out to be no document, barely cold, though removed now from the sacks and the summerhouse, he's suffered the last of his indignities, has had his very identity stripped from him, is now not Clooney, perhaps not American, only certainly alone. Alone, and unnamed. A piece of carrion with no handle. Shorn of all points of departure from which to imagine something, anything, to clothe his great nakedness. No name, no nation, no birthplace, no domicile, no shared culture, no relatives, no friends, nothing. X, torn from his equation. From his short masquerade. His make-believe. His attitude of separation, of maintaining a distinct ego. X, a dangerous picture, the residuum left in the crucible.

So Grosvenor Square ring Whitehall with this news of non-identity, requiring at the same time, now or sooner, a very close description of X; his height, weight, colouring, marks, teeth, prints, estimated age, together with information of his accent and manner, when he was alive, and all other information whatever; with the precise mode of his dying, and preferably the names of those responsible. Whitehall reply with polite brevity, having none of this information by them, then ring the local H.Q., who in turn ring the beleaguered Shelton. Shelton, by now, is beginning to appreciate the weight of the pyramid he is supporting, and he counters H.Q. with a request for assistance. Alas for Shelton! This day he has shed many illusions. He has been pushed around by a bunch of reporters who have found out a good deal more than he has. It was they, not he, who discovered the hotel was locked up by 11.30 p.m., and that the guests, all *forty-four* of them, and the staff, could each show themselves to have been inside it. It was they, not he, who elicited that the American set out, it must be, after 10 p.m., as he did by habit, always alone, usually northward along the cliffs. It was not that Shelton would not have made these discoveries, but that he did not get the chance, there being only one Shelton, assisted by his sergeant, as against fourteen reporters; fourteen reporters, furthermore, who knew what to ask as well as Shelton, and wasted no time in asking it, or in collating the answers. And yet, after all, it is not very much, removed from the context of banner headlines, and promises to lead to no more in the useful future. Rather it is scraping the bottom, of which Shelton is miserably aware; it is likely no one will ever know more, or very much more, than he does at present. It may even be that the lonely American did indeed slay himself. Hence, being found in this frame of mind, Shelton makes a quick decision: he has done his best, in the limits and conditions, and if more is required, let others come after it, and because his point of view, so stated, would find no favour with authority, he translates it into an irresistible form: I'll need more men. What for? At least, to let him start level with the press! To enable him, within a reasonable time, to cope with three-score-and-ten interrogations. Though, as Shelton craftily insinuates, it will probably be winnowing chaff only, he has no reason to anticipate, as it leaves him, that further interrogations will produce anything. Pause, discussion at H.Q. Has he, H.Q. asks, come to any conclusion? Not a conclusion, Shelton replies hastily, but a feeling, you know how it is, that if anyone did murder the American, which is far from being established, then that someone is outside the scope of the present inquiries. Not a local person, Shelton says daringly, nobody in the hotel or the village. Someone out of the American's past. If the American, indeed, were murdered. More discussion at H.Q. Have you found the weapon? H.Q. ask. Shelton is obliged to admit he hasn't, though he has had Stody tramping the cliff-top all day. Any thoughts about that? H.Q. ask. Shelton has many thoughts about that. In the first place, he has dragged out of Halliday the general proposition that suicides often try two or more methods. Thus it is far from unlikely that the twenty-two incisions were self-inflicted, a sort of bungled hara-kiri, which the American had not the courage to consummate; while as for the weapon, Halliday agreed that a piece of broken glass would suffice, and Shelton himself, on an excursion along the cliff-top, had counted eight discarded bottles, two of them broken. Any glass he might have used? Not exactly, but it proved nothing. He may have made the incisions somewhere else, say on the beach, where there were also bottles. Then, if it chanced to have been on the foreshore where the American abandoned his bloodied glass, the next tide would have removed it, buried it, or if neither of these, at least unbloodied it. Shrewd Shelton! What a plausible picture he is building up for H.Q., or rather, letting H.Q. draw from him, goaded by his request for more men. The cleverer, because H.Q. will want to believe it, to cut the case down to coroner-size, to return Shelton to his breaking-and-enterings and to keep the crime record tidy. On the one hand, sensational murder, straining resources and offering no credit; on the other, a routine suicide, with credit to Shelton for pricking the bubble. Can they hesitate? Not for long! Report back in, they tell Shelton.

So Shelton has been clever, Shelton has an explanation for everything, except, and Stody annoyingly put it in his report, Stody's reservation about it being dark, and except certain bruises on the body which may, or may not, offend the coroner. Stody's point is a good one. The American must needs have projected himself from the cliff-top. Yet if it were dark (and the night was moonless), how could he have aimed so precisely at the pill-box? Had he been anticipating the jump during his stay at the hotel, directing his stroll to the spot each evening, measuring, calculating the event? So much so, that on a night when the pill-box below was invisible, he could yet, exactly, position himself, and, exactly, leap over? Incredible, not to be believed; except for the rude, unwinking fact. Yet, as Shelton is quick to see, the difficulty is no objection to a concept of suicide, because if murder is postulated, the difficulty remains, as much for the murderer as for the American. If not X, then Y must have measured and calculated; and Y (O Shelton!) would have had the greater difficulty, having to heave another, and not himself. So that, if any conclusion is to be drawn (thus Shelton, on the wings of inspiration), it is that Stody's point, if it can't be ignored, by a feather, favours suicide. Fine reasoning, and H.Q. is half-disposed to accept it. But there are still the bruises outstanding, and Shelton must reason around those too. And here Shelton's inspiration flags, because the bruises' story is so obvious, saying to him, as to any policeman, This man was held down, with a knee on his chest. Ignore them? Brazen it out with the coroner? H.Q. shakes its head regretfully. Suppose . . . Shelton supposes hard, can make no contact with the divine spark. It lies with the bruises, H.Q. says, everything stands or falls by them; we can't pretend they were self-inflicted; they are evidence of an attacker. But – a thousand things, Shelton says, an attacker may not have been a murderer, it may have been (inspiration flickers bravely), may have been an attack that triggered off the suicide. You have evidence of this, H.Q. says. There is no evidence either way, Shelton pleads, and furthermore a man can bruise his own wrists, as, for example, by struggling while in hand-cuffs. You have evidence –, H.Q. begins, but Shelton knows he has shot his bolt, is even (he is a good policeman) beginning to realize that his defence of suicide is an indictment of it. There's a case to answer, and he knows it, has all this time played the devil's advocate, would dearly have loved to have got away with it, finds the bruises blocking his way. Right, he says, like Stody before him: he is re-aligned with the formula. But if it's murder, he says, he's getting nowhere, and has a strong suspicion there's nowhere to get, unless (and provided the murderer is a hotel inmate), unless someone breaks down under interrogation. Because the picture there is formidable, a picture of credible cross-alibis, with no pointer, not one, connecting the American with any individual. He is a stray bird who flew down there, a rare exotic, strangely plumaged, viewed suspiciously by the resident birds and common migrants alike, tolerated, because he was quiet, and permitted to pick a little with the others, but making no friends, no enemies; probably pining; at last, dying. He had no handle, that American! He had given a vague London address in the register. He had on him money enough to pay his bill, but no indication of where more would come from. You'd say he'd simply come there to die, to die unknown and untraceable: so well would suicide fit the bill, if he'd kept his wrists away from bruises. And if no connection, no motive. Not a shade of a motive has Shelton uncovered. X remains unqualified, no sign stands against him, no suggestion of mode of relation with a postulated Y. If indeed the equation exists, it is remote from our knowledge, Shelton avers.

Then – and Shelton and H.Q. both know it must come: they have only talked so long to clear the ground – with suicide out, or at least questionable, what remains but to kick the case upstairs? Oh, a show of reluctance on both sides! – Sorry, Shelton, but you see how it is. Just one of those things, sir, it happens to the best of us. – After you've done all the donkey-work. – We have to work as a team, sir. A decent disguise for mutual relief: when H.Q. can lift the phone, and, metaphorically, boot the can into the blue distance. The formula provides for it, and the law allows it. Whitehall listens to H.Q. with Whitehall's usual condescension (have they not seen, with their wary eyes, innumerable cans arrive from the provinces?) and ask questions which are half questions, half insinuations of H.Q.'s naïveté, until they have the facts, the whole facts, nailed immovable for instant reference. Then, strange – most strange! – they begin to argue somewhat like Shelton, though with, in place of Shelton's wistful pleading, a tone of uncontradictable authority, showing how, on the facts rehearsed, on the balance of the facts, the case is suicide, and that H.Q. will do well to wrest this verdict, by correct presentation, from the coroner. Amazement, alarm, in H.Q.! They summon their wits to do battle. The can, hovering invisibly above the wires, speeds now this way, now that. Through fire and brimstone, storm and wrack, H.Q. maintains the cause of the bruises, though assaulted before, beside and behind by the nimble fencer of Whitehall. The bruises, always is their cry, and bloodied but firm, still they cry it. And finally that cry deafens Whitehall, and the can settles a little Londonwards. Continue investigations, Whitehall says, we will confer with the American authorities, it may be, could be, is just possible, that the man has a record that supports your contention. We, for our part, consider it unlikely, but we appreciate your concern. Please keep us informed of any developments. Please give only general statements to the press. Message ends, and H.Q. are uncertain whether they have won or lost the battle. But Whitehall, wiping a little blood from its rapier, knows where the can has come to rest. In course, having now the requested details, they do confer with the American authorities, but the American authorities, after considering the details, are no wiser than before. They'll check it out for the British, naturally, whether X is or is not their national; but right now they can say for sure he is on no list held by them;

and the British, they insinuate, would be well advised to keep an open mind on X's nationality, thereby not hindering their investigations by possibly unwarranted reservations. Yes, Whitehall says, yes, and stifles a very polite sigh. Then Whitehall glances at a duty list and makes a few quick calculations. A phone is lifted, a phone rings. There is a departmental query. Gently is your man, says department, Chief Superintendent George Gently. Tell him to report, Whitehall says. And Chief Superintendent Gently reports.

CHAPTER FOUR

A LL THIS OCCUPIES one day after the death of the lonely American – or X, as he now becomes, pending more curious inquiry – a fine and particular day in July, with temperatures pushing the eighties, and a shore breeze turning into a sea breeze, and the Hotel Continental's windows all open. No music there today, not even the most melancholy. No sound of zither, fiddle, accordion, mingling with the soft-murmuring combers. Mrs Breske stays in her room. Trudi Breske refrains from tennis. Frieda, more sombre but not less efficient, undertakes the hotel routine, alone. And the guests – don't know what to do about it, after talking the affair to a standstill; by evening the guests are very bored, and wish the American had died elsewhere. True, the service hasn't suffered, apart from the article of music, and no one has made any prohibitions, which the knowing half-expected; yet, and still, they feel bored, as though something promised has failed to develop, as though a breathless vision of the extraordinary has tailed away into commonplace. They feel guilty, but not guilty enough.

They are all too certain of being spectators. X, or the American, may have to do with the Breskes, or some unimaginable unknown, but not with themselves. Academically they are suspects, but no more, and their certain innocence is irksome; yet they cannot return to the established tenor which X, or the American, interrupted. They are suspended, are in a vacuum, or are, in one word, bored. Not even the weather or the evening papers can entirely conceal this grinding truth.

So they sleep, and so they wake; when lo! – a man is in their midst; a man immediately recognizable as Someone by the attention of the reporters; a large man, with big shoulders, with a square face and troubling eyes, looking mentally and physically equipped, as he is, to be the support of giant pyramids: where Stody wilted and Shelton paled, see here Chief Superintendent Gently. Shelton is with him, but Shelton knows his supernumerary status. He hangs back, permits Gently to cut his swathe through the pressmen. And this the mighty man does, like a king moving among his suppliants, and they, the terror of poor Shelton, press not too close upon his majesty. His name is whispered, and the guests have heard it. They are in the presence of a manner of hero. One whose occupation is with death, with many deaths, with death in terror. They stare at Gently, this modern hero, this man who opens up mysteries, whose strong hands, casually filling a pipe, have ripped the veil from many a dying: who has seen what they pray not to see, has dealt with men they pray not to deal with: makes, as vocation, a common thing, what most men fear and turn aside from: at him they stare, a modern hero, a man who occupies himself with death. And he unthinkingly stares back, seeing the straw he will make his bricks with, mindlessly noting a thousand things as he tells the reporters precisely nothing, quite unaware within himself of the projection of a heroic image, which he would immediately know to be false, though it would reveal to him much about those who perceived it. He stares, and eyes fall, though his stare is a mild one. His stare has no penetration, yet it seems to lay one open. He has greenish-hazel eyes that lie peaceably beneath thick brows, but they have some odd power of irradiating people, of setting them in a brilliant light. He sees all round you. You cannot hide from him. No shadow is left to conceal a deception. But all this is serene, has no aggression, is almost shared or exchanged with you. Strange, naked-seeing eyes! What wonder that other eyes fall before them?

The reporters disperse; they have all he'll give them, and they know better than to ask for more. Gently says a few words to Shelton, Shelton, who almost jumps to attention. Listen a moment, Shelton says fiercely, we want statements from all you people. We'll try to get through them as quickly as possible, but I want no one going out before they've made their statement. Is that clear? Perfectly clear! The guests admire Shelton's new note of authority. Right, says Shelton (God bless the formula!), we'll be taking the statements in the office. Then he, and his sergeant, Walters, and a shorthand-writer, Policewoman Dicks, set up shop in the tiny office behind the desk, beneath the alpenhorn; which office, having glass-panelled walls, shows that no deception is intended. But the man himself, the great panjandrum, is he not to be of their number? Apparently not. He pays no attention to the inquisition in the office. He goes outside, comes back inside, makes a tour of the rooms, the stairs, the kitchens, as though he suspects each and all of these to have a close bearing on the death of the American; and in a curious way, by doing this, he makes it seem not the least improbable, so that those who see him begin to peer about too and to search for guilt in familiar things. Then, having made everyone uneasy, and said something in Italian to the waiter Carlo, he goes through the big carved door lettered: *Eingang Verboten*, behind which is Mrs Breske's private parlour suite. And so is lost to the eyes of the guests, who yet feel a great deal less innocent than when he arrived.

Mrs Breske is in her parlour. She is sitting in a rocking-chair by the window. Her big face is puffy and suety and sagging and her mouth, partly open, shows uneven teeth. She has a trace of moustache and a wart on her chin from which the hair grows bushily. The hair of her head, still dark, is parted in the centre and is perfectly straight. She rocks herself. She moans. She stares before her with bulbous grey eyes. She is wearing a widow's dress, entirely black, with short sleeves which are too tight for her. A thick, podgy woman with rolling breasts and plump calves, and a tendency to drift into spells of abstraction: this is Edith Breske at fifty. She starts when she hears Gently's knock. She calls, Herein! – and struggles from the chair. Gently, entering, begs her not to rise, and she falls back in the chair, which oscillates dumbly. Herr Inspektor – Superintendent. Ach, in my country that is Inspektor. Gently smiles. He has a winning smile. Edith Breske feels she may like him. Will you not sit yourself, Herr Inspektor? Gently chooses a frail, painted chair: there are six of these, and a matching sofa, with a scene from a boar-hunt embroidered on the back-rest. The carpet also, pale, fine-piled, depicts scenes of hawking and hunting, with ruffled men in tricorn hats astride small but fiery, caracoling, horses. A very fine carpet, yes, is true? Gently admits it is very fine. You like my furniture? Gently likes it. Ach, it cost Edith Breske a great deal of money. The carpet, the chairs, the sofa were once the property of Prinz Josef Czynska – you know, related to the Hohenlohe-Schillingsfürsts, and so, of need, to Maria Theresa? Gently confesses to not knowing this, yet Edith Breske affirms it; feels now established aboon her might, and at least on a level with Herr Inspektor. But what can she tell him, that she has not told already, to that other, inferior, Herr Unterinspektor?

GENTLY

I want you to tell me, Mrs Breske, everything you remember about the deceased.

MRS BRESKE

But there is nothing! He is here six, seven weeks, and I do not speak to him more than twice.

GENTLY

Did he have an accent?

MRS BRESKE

Ach, yes. He came from America, is true. He has that slur, you know, and he speaks through his nose. I, myself, have met many Americans. During the War I was in London. This one, yes, he is like the others, indeed, is certain.

GENTLY

He had a strong accent?

MRS BRESKE

Oh, ja.

GENTLY

Perhaps a little too strong?

MRS BRESKE

How is that?

GENTLY

His accent impressed you though he spoke so little. Perhaps the accent was a fake.

MRS BRESKE

(And she is stirred by this, her eyes swelling, her hands thrusting; her hands, on the thickened ring finger of which she still wears a fat gold band.)

Is not so, I tell you! He is an American from New York. His clothes too, his face, his ways – why should I tell you what is not so? Ask Frieda, she will tell you. I do not lie about this.

GENTLY

(Shrugs.)

Just an idea. Why did he come to your hotel?

MRS BRESKE

Why? How should I know that? Why do other people come?

GENTLY

Have other Americans stayed here?

MRS BRESKE

No. My clients are English people.

GENTLY

No other nationalities – say Austrians?

MRS BRESKE

I do not remember. Ask Frieda.

GENTLY

Then surely you'd be rather interested in this one, your first, American. You'd want to give him a good impression. And in fact, he did stay on for six weeks?

MRS BRESKE

I cannot help about that. He is just a guest like other people. He say, It suit me, is what I want, I will stay on: like that.

GENTLY

He owed you nothing?

MRS BRESKE

Ach, no!

GENTLY

He always paid you in English money?

MRS BRESKE

In English money, ja.

GENTLY

No travellers' cheques?

MRS BRESKE

(Shakes her head.)

GENTLY

Didn't you wonder what he was doing here, staying on from week to week – no letters, no contacts; just idling away his time?

MRS BRESKE

It is his business, what he does.

GENTLY

But you'd have made some remark. You'd have said: You're having a long holiday, Mr Clooney, some little thing like that.

MRS BRESKE

(She rocks the chair, her eyes protruding and distant. The impression you have is that her soul has departed, is perhaps wandering the streets of pre-war Vienna.)

GENTLY

Well?

MRS BRESKE

Ja, some little thing. I try to remember myself. About his wife, I say that. That she will wonder where he is got to.

GENTLY

And what did he say?

MRS BRESKE

Ach, a joke. Yes, he is laughing, I remember. She is going, mmn, mmn, with other men, she will not wonder about him.

GENTLY

But he admitted having a wife.

MRS BRESKE

I tell you, it was a joke.

GENTLY

Was he . . . bitter, about it?

MRS BRESKE

No, not that one. He does not care, you understand?

GENTLY

Would you say he had something on his mind.

MRS BRESKE

He does not care about his wife. He laughs, he has jokes about her, is all over long ago. Ach, poor woman, whoever she is! I know. I know.

(And Edith Breske is absent again, this time certainly in Vienna, waltzing again with that romantic fiddler, that Martin Breske, her first and falsest.)

GENTLY

Are you a widow, Mrs Breske?

MRS BRESKE

Ach, who can tell me that? He ran off to Berlin with a blonde hair-dresser. Perhaps the Nazis got hold of him. He was, you know – was ist ein Schmetterling?

GENTLY

Butterfly.

41

MRS BRESKE

Ja, ein butterfly. A woman can do what she likes with him, he has no character, is a child. But good-looking, ach yes! I do not wish him any evil.

GENTLY

Your two daughters are very unlike.

MRS BRESKE

(Sharply.)

They are both his, that is true. Trudi takes after her father, is nothing erstaunlich about that.

GENTLY

He was tall, then.

MRS BRESKE

Ja, ja, he was not altogether short. Und Trudi has his eyes, his nose, ja, is very much like him.

GENTLY

(Pointing.)

Would that be his sister on that photograph?

MRS BRESKE

(Turning quickly, so that the chair swings.)

Was ist – nein, nein, er hat keine Schwester – jene ist Frau Lindemann – sie ist tot.

GENTLY

A relative?

MRS BRESKE

Oh, ja. She is my sister, Mitzi Lindemann. She married Herr Professor Hermann Lindemann. They are both dead before the war.

Then that's where Trudi gets her looks.

MRS BRESKE

Ja, is possible, is in the family. The Nazis killed Herr Professor. He is born the wrong side of the bridge.

GENTLY

What bridge?

MRS BRESKE

The Radetsky Bridge. Das heisst, he is a Jew. Also, he is known to be a Marxist. Is enough. They shoot him.

GENTLY

And your sister?

MRS BRESKE
(Shrugs.)

She is already sick at that time. Ach, what do you know in your island? The sea out there is still all round you.

She snatches her head and stares, protuberantly, at the same circumfluent sea, where it lies, patched with emerald, purple and gamboge, but hard blue, beyond her window. Edith Breske, who had seen no sea till those nightmare months of '37, to whom it is, will ever be, a roaring desert of separation; never soothing, never inviting, but God's mighty current dividing the land. She stares, daughter of muddy Danube, alien-eyed, at prison bars.

GENTLY

So perhaps the American had a wife. That is all you can tell me about him. Now, Mrs Breske, I want you to remember what you can about Tuesday evening. Did you see the American go out?

MRS BRESKE
(Shakes her head.)
I see the poor man at dinner. After that, I don't know. I think I do not see him again.

GENTLY
Who sat at his table?

MRS BRESKE
He has a table by himself.

GENTLY
Always?

MRS BRESKE
Ja, always. He ask for the little window table.

GENTLY
That's the window overlooking the drive.

MRS BRESKE
Ja, and he has the room just above it. At first I give him a front room, but he says the noise of the sea keep him awake. That is all right, other people like it, I am quite happy he shall move.

GENTLY
So he had a room and a table overlooking the drive. It was almost as though he expected a visitor.

MRS BRESKE
(Hoists her shoulders.)

GENTLY

Did he have one?

MRS BRESKE

A thousand times I tell you, no! He is alone, that man. He does not talk, make friends. He sits in his room, walks on the beach, eats his food, listens to the music. You do not know he is there. He does not make any complaint. He seems content, he smiles at you. But he does not open his mouth.

GENTLY

Did that never strike you as odd?

MRS BRESKE

Odd? Himmel, they are all odd! I am too busy, I do not notice. Ach, he pays his bill, nicht wahr?

GENTLY

But you did notice.

MRS BRESKE

Is all the same! Other people are funny too.

GENTLY

Not quite so funny.

MRS BRESKE

Pfoo, pfoo.

GENTLY

Are they?

MRS BRESKE
(An impatient gesture.)

Going back to Tuesday evening. You saw the American at dinner. Who served him?

MRS BRESKE

Ja – Franz. Franz is serving the little table.

GENTLY

Who is he?

MRS BRESKE

Who? A waiter. Franz Klapper. Is from Ischl.

GENTLY

A regular waiter?

MRS BRESKE

Oh, ja. Is here from two, three seasons.

GENTLY

What time would you have finished dinner?

MRS BRESKE

Ach, the service is over at nine. But people sit there, you know, there is the music, good wine. Till ten or eleven it is sometimes. The orchestra go off at eleven.

GENTLY

And the American kept sitting there?

MRS BRESKE

I do not know that myself. Frieda says he is still there at a quarter past ten.

GENTLY

Drinking?

MRS BRESKE

Ja, that is certain. He is served six whiskies.

GENTLY

He listens to the music, and drinks.

MRS BRESKE

Ja. It is his way.

Gently is silent. Mrs Breske slides a look at him. Is not so terrible, this Herr Oberinspektor, though perhaps shrewd, ach yes! Now he arranges in his capacious mind (does he not resemble the great Willi, that chef, the favourite of crowned heads, whose disciple she is proud to be; who, as she is fond of telling, could break two dozen eggs in twenty seconds, the shells falling in a neat pile in a pan placed there to receive them – One does not break eggs, Fraulein Tichtel, one introduces them – ?) her words, not one of which he has forgotten or failed to give its full significance. What then? He can make nothing of them to the discredit of Edith Breske, or of the Hotel Continental, its staff, and its forty-four guests. He will ask his fill, no doubt, and write a long, highly official report, which will satisfy everybody concerned, and tie the matter up neatly; that is his business as a Herr Oberinspektor; but he can do no more. The great Willi, without eggs, could not make a Spanish omelette. Mrs Breske stares large-eyed, rocks sedately, waits.

GENTLY

So then the American goes out.

MRS BRESKE

Ja, he often does this before retiring.

47

GENTLY

Always alone.

MRS BRESKE

Is what they say. I do not myself keep late hours.

GENTLY

When did you retire, Mrs Breske?

MRS BRESKE

Ach, nine, a half after. It is very tiring, you understand,
I am a long time in the kitchen.

GENTLY

And then?

MRS BRESKE

Ja?

GENTLY

What followed?

MRS BRESKE

(Stares at him, her teeth showing.)

GENTLY

When you had gone up, what followed?

MRS BRESKE

Was? I undress, go to bed!

GENTLY

And then?

MRS BRESKE

Then? Ich weiss nicht! – what do you mean, and then?

GENTLY

(Shakes his head.)

MRS BRESKE

(Her mouth crumples.)

GENTLY

It won't do, Mrs Breske. This is a murder investigation.
I have to know what people were doing, how far they
can be eliminated. You told Inspector Shelton you slept
alone. The waiter, Gordini, says he slept alone. Other
people have said you slept together. If you did, you must
tell me.

MRS BRESKE

(In tears.)

Is not fair to ask this!

GENTLY

Don't forget it clears Gordini.

MRS BRESKE

(Passionately.)

Ach, Carlo! As though you believe – ! What could
Carlo know about this?

GENTLY

(Shrugs.)

He's a strong boy, perhaps has a knife.

MRS BRESKE

Ach, Gott, Sie sind verrückt! Next it is me, is Trudi, is
Frieda – are plenty of knives in the kitchen!

GENTLY

So.

MRS BRESKE
(Crying.)

Is not fair! Why must I tell you? Carlo is gentle, like an angel. Franz, ja, he has a temper – but Carlo, Carlo! Is all madness!

GENTLY
(Waits.)

MRS BRESKE
(Still crying.)
Carlo is kind, you understand?

GENTLY
I haven't accused him.

MRS BRESKE
Carlo loves me. Ach, a woman needs to be loved! You ask if I am a widow. Ja, jawohl, I am a widow! All these years I have no husband, no one to sleep at my side. Is too much, is not right, a woman cannot do like that.

GENTLY
I'm not here to blame you, Mrs Breske.

MRS BRESKE
She needs a man, all the time. Is not alive, you understand, is not living, without a man. Ach, to be a lonely woman! How can one tell a man of this? Is nothing inside her, is all hollow. Without loving is no good!

GENTLY
Well.

MRS BRESKE
Is not right! You do not need to ask this.

GENTLY

I must know your movements.

MRS BRESKE

Oh, ja, ja!

GENTLY

You saw as much of the American as anyone.

MRS BRESKE

(She dashes angrily at the tears on her tallowy cheeks, seems about to give an explosive answer, then, surprisingly does not.)

Are all the same, diese Polizisten. English, deutsch, it does not matter.

GENTLY

Gordini slept with you, didn't he.

MRS BRESKE

Gut, so! What then?

GENTLY

When did he come, when did he leave?

MRS BRESKE

Und was tat er dort, you would like to know?

GENTLY

Just what I'm asking.

MRS BRESKE

Oh, ja. He brought up my night-cap, it is ten hours.

GENTLY

And stayed.

51

MRS BRESKE

Ja, and slept.

GENTLY

Till.

MRS BRESKE

Ach, I am not sure. Is all this business, everyone awake. He was in my room till after six hours.

GENTLY

From ten p.m. to six a.m.

MRS BRESKE

Ja, is certain, I can say.

GENTLY

That's all about that, Mrs Breske. Thank you for being frank with me.

MRS BRESKE

(Does not look very grateful for Gently's thanks. She makes a manner of humming sound through her nose, rather like an angry cat.)

GENTLY

(As though half to himself.)

Of course . . . all this was very upsetting for you.

MRS BRESKE

You do not care about that. People's feelings do not matter.

GENTLY

But you were upset, weren't you?

MRS BRESKE

Ach, Gott, am I not to be? One of my guests has been
killed – a good advertisement is it, ja?

GENTLY

And this it was that upset you?

MRS BRESKE

Is not enough? Ach, this man!

GENTLY

But wasn't it making matters worse – to be hysterical
over it in front of your guests?

MRS BRESKE

(Gapes for a moment.)
I cry a little, nothing more! This man is killed who I
have known – I cry, ja – I have my feelings.

GENTLY

So it wasn't just the bad advertisement.

MRS BRESKE

Ja – nein! I am not a stone.

GENTLY

Yet you spoke to him only twice.

MRS BRESKE

Es macht nichts – is my way!

GENTLY

(A faint shrug.)
Perhaps, without noticing, you had become fond of
him.

MRS BRESKE

Nein, I tell you – I do not care! Is nothing to me, is only a guest – Number 7, does not complain.

GENTLY

But you cry.

MRS BRESKE

Ach, ach!

GENTLY

Could it be you were afraid?

MRS BRESKE

(Says nothing, rocks her chair, stares, showing her bunched teeth.)

GENTLY

You may remember something later on. People often do that. Now I'd like to talk to some other people, Mrs Breske. First, I think, to your daughter.

MRS BRESKE

Ja . . . Frieda.

GENTLY

Yes.

MRS BRESKE

I will find her, send her to you.

CHAPTER FIVE

A ND NOW MRS Breske, leaving her parlour, coming into the hall, where guests sit waiting, is much less easy in her mind about the Herr Oberinspektor and his shrewdness: so much so that her first act, after scowling distantly at the guests, is to enter the bar and to order a neat brandy from Rudi, the bartender. She drinks it quickly. Ach, Rudi! Rudi is a youngster from Hochstadt-bei-Zoom. He has brown eyes and a bee-stung mouth and may one day serve night-caps. Ach, Rudi! Ja, 'dige Frau? Mrs Breske shakes her head. She cannot put her uneasiness in words, either English or German. And Rudi gazes at her doe-eyed, troubled by Frau Breske's trouble, wondering if the occasion of it is some sin or omission of his own. You knew the American, Rudi? Absurd question! Of course he did. So? Another shake of the head. Ach, Rudi! – is all. Then she stands turning the brandy-glass, looking at Rudi without seeing him, till the lad becomes embarrassed and starts to blush round the ears. What is the matter with Frau Breske? Rudi is used to a different approach.

She goes then, warmed by brandy, into the kitchen, holy of holies! where fowls are browning in the big ovens, and an assistant chef makes strudel pastry. Here she is queen and in her realm; she snuffs the super-heated air. Frieda, her face ashine, is slicing melons with a large knife. Ach, Frieda! That strain again! Frieda lays the knife by. The assistant chef slaps and slaps at pastry already semi-transparent. The kitchen-boy, in his corner, is feeding potatoes into a whirring machine, while the second assistant chef, as though he hates them, is chopping herbs on a board. Noise, heat, smell! Frieda – hsst! I have been with the policeman. What have you told him? Not so loud! He is like a gimlet, that Inspektor. You have said nothing – Ach, nichts! But he goes about it as one plucks a chicken – fuff, fuff, off come the feathers; you are turned and twisted every way. Quick, hissed words between mother and daughter. Frieda picks up the knife again, the pointed knife with the straight back. As they talk she slices. The green melons are carved in segments. A sweep of the knife clears the seeds, the knife undercuts, scores the meat. A busy, expert, delicate knife, with a sharp, simple, strong blade, slicing, sweeping, flicking, scoring while Frieda listens and questions. Now he will see you. – In good time. Watch him Frieda, ach, watch him! A pity – Ja! The knife flickers. Still noise, heat, smell. And Frieda goes, when the melons are ready, not bothering to remove her overall coat, not bothering to powder her shiny face: she wipes her hands and goes. Ach, Rudi, ach, Frieda! You could cut the heat with Frieda's knife. The brandy beads on Frau Breske's nose and she swims in the balm of roasting poultry.

Frieda taps and enters the parlour, carrying some poultry flavour with her. Poultry flavour encroaches on the regular parlour-essence of lavender polish and stale roses. Gently is standing at the end of the parlour, a figure too large for that fragile room, examining the photographs on the what-not, the painted, gilded what-not, ex-Prinz Czynska. Your mother has nice things, he says, you have a good trade here. Frieda moves driftingly a few steps, says nothing, looks nothing. These silver frames, Gently says, this pair of figures – aren't they Dresden? – and the Nattier picture in the carved frame, which looks so well between Sèvres vases . . . Frieda looks at them, barely shrugs. Perhaps they don't interest you, Gently says. Frieda shrugs again. They are mother's things, she buys them to remind her of old times. Buys them where? In Vienna, where else? She goes there each autumn to visit her father. Has she other relatives, connections, there? No: just her father: the others are dead. And you, Gently says, do you visit Vienna? Frieda shakes her head. What is that place to her? She prefers the London of her childhood, and Leicester Square to the Ring. Yes, there is London in plain Frieda, her eyes light a little when she speaks of it, her grey, mother's eyes which, however, do not protrude. She has been to Vienna, though? Yes, Trudi and she were there once. She liked it? Well . . . in fact, she was bored. Her mother had been miserable all the trip. They had visited a number of dingy streets and spoken to a number of dreary people, that was what she remembered chiefly about the City of Dreams. That, and the Danube being brown. Vienna was really nothing special. Here Frieda stops, glances quickly at Gently, is

57

alarmed at finding herself speaking freely. Gently apparently notices nothing. He is just taking his pipe from his pocket. May he smoke? Of course. He fills his pipe. Frieda is silent.

GENTLY

Take a seat, Miss Breske.

FRIEDA

(Sits near the window. She folds her hands on her lap, lets her eyes stray through the window.)

GENTLY

(Sitting.)
Is that Trudi we can see, playing tennis?

FRIEDA

Yes.

GENTLY

Who's the young man with her?

FRIEDA

Stephen. Doctor Halliday's nephew.

GENTLY

Her boy-friend?

FRIEDA

I wouldn't know. You'd better ask Trudi.

GENTLY

She's attractive, your sister.

FRIEDA

(Says nothing.)

GENTLY

Well now, Miss Breske, I think you may be able to help me. You do the book-keeping, don't you, so you'll have talked to Wilbur Clooney.

FRIEDA

I have only spoken business to him.

GENTLY

Of course. But you'll have learned something from that. For instance, when his wallet was out, you'd notice if it was thin or fat.

FRIEDA

(Hesitates.)

GENTLY

You did notice?

FRIEDA

I think he had plenty in it.

GENTLY

Plenty?

FRIEDA

I couldn't see how much, could I? But the wallet always looked bulky.

GENTLY

It wasn't so bulky when he was found. There was money in it, but not a lot.

FRIEDA

I don't know anything about that. I'm telling you about when I saw it.

This could be important, Miss Breske. I'd like you to think very carefully. Let's see, he'd have paid you on Saturday, wouldn't he? How did his wallet look then?

FRIEDA

I don't remember.

GENTLY

You saw it, didn't you?

FRIEDA

I may have done. I don't know.

GENTLY

Didn't he pay you?

FRIEDA

Oh yes! I think he just handed me the money.

GENTLY

The exact sum.

FRIEDA

Yes – no, I may have given him some change.

GENTLY

I see. But at other times you noticed his wallet looking bulky.

FRIEDA

I think so, yes. But it needn't have been money.

Gently looks pleased, Frieda Breske less so. She is perhaps beginning to wish she had powdered her shine, had removed her chicken-redolent overall. She smoothes back a straggle of lifeless hair with a deft, secretive movement. Gently puffs a little. His tobacco has a piny, mannish smell.

GENTLY

No, it needn't have been money. That's one of the oddities of the case. He seems to have come here with just enough money to see him through till he was murdered. Unless, of course, he was getting supplies — drawing a weekly sum from somewhere. But he had no mail, nothing in the safe, spoke to no one, made no trips.

FRIEDA

Perhaps after all he killed himself.

GENTLY

Perhaps.

FRIEDA

He may have had money to draw on. When he had finished what he had with him. If he had lived, he might have gone after it.

GENTLY

He told you that?

FRIEDA

Of course not!

GENTLY

But something gave you that idea.

FRIEDA

It could have been like that, couldn't it?

GENTLY

Oh yes.

FRIEDA

It's a suggestion, that's all. Actually, he did mention expecting a letter.

GENTLY

Oh, he did expect one, did he?

FRIEDA

Yes, he told me he was expecting one, an important letter, it was on Saturday.

GENTLY

But no letter has come.

FRIEDA

(Shakes her head.)

GENTLY

Yet.

FRIEDA

He didn't say when.

GENTLY

But we can assume it will arrive soon.

FRIEDA

(Says nothing.)

GENTLY

Yet supposing there was no letter: no contacts, no letter. Just this odd American living on here, with always money enough to pay his bill. Pocket money, subsistence money, but no apparent outside supply. Sufficient money on him when he dies, but no more than sufficient. What does that suggest to you?

FRIEDA

I don't know, it's a mystery.

GENTLY

But what would make it less a mystery?

FRIEDA

I tell you, I don't know.

GENTLY

It would be less of a mystery to me if someone here supplied him with money. Yet who could that be?

FRIEDA

I've already told you—

GENTLY

Of course. You don't know.

Frieda pouts. There is faint colour in her pasty cheeks. She is holding herself in, but one has the impression of violence not far below the surface. She would like to fly at this detective, to send him smarting about his business; but she cannot. That is the impression. Some little matter bars the way.

GENTLY

So, on Tuesday evening, you see him go out.

FRIEDA

I've told the other man all that.

About seeing him leave?

I didn't say that! I said I saw him at a quarter past ten.

That's the latest he was seen by anyone, he must have gone out soon after. Where was he, what was he doing?

He was in the dining-room. He was drinking.

Just that?

He always drank. He sat at his table reading a paper. I didn't notice him particularly, he was just there. As usual.

Was anyone near him?

Nobody. Most of them were sitting on the lawn.

Any of the staff?

Not near him. Franz and Johann were stripping the tables.

You noticed nothing unusual about him.

FRIEDA

Nothing at all. He was just sitting there. He'd go out
by the french door near his table, that's why no one saw
him leave.

GENTLY

It was all very usual, and his usual time.

FRIEDA

Yes. He never went out till dark.

Gently puffs a little more, staring over the lawns at the
sea, the sea which, at its horizon, is now a burning haze
of azure, over the tennis court where lithe Trudi is
skilfully banging back returns, where the doctor's
nephew calls the score, where some escaped guests sit
watching. His eyes appear absent, or perhaps full of the
sea.

GENTLY

Why didn't you like Clooney, Miss Breske?

FRIEDA

(Surprised into glancing at him.)
I haven't said I didn't like him.

GENTLY

But you didn't.

FRIEDA

Well, if I didn't. He wasn't much of a man.

GENTLY

Did he make a pass at you?

FRIEDA

Him!

GENTLY

He must have been rather bored here.

FRIEDA

Thank you very much, but men don't have to be bored to make passes at me.

GENTLY

Perhaps you made one at him.

FRIEDA

Really, that's quite enough!

GENTLY

He did something to upset you. Or didn't do something.

FRIEDA

He was ugly. Old and ugly. He was a yank. He talked like a moron. He drank, wore vulgar clothes. Isn't that enough why I didn't like him?

GENTLY

He wasn't so old and ugly . . .

FRIEDA

Yes, old and ugly. Perhaps not to you, but to me. I couldn't stand him. That's flat.

GENTLY

No other reason.

FRIEDA

None.

GENTLY

Like him staying on, and staying on.

FRIEDA

That was his business. He paid, didn't he?

GENTLY

(Doesn't say anything.)

FRIEDA

Him making a pass – that's filthy! A crude old boozer like that. You don't know what you are saying. He might have been my grandfather.

GENTLY

He was fifty-one.

FRIEDA

My father then. But too old! He stank of drink. Ask Rudi. His nose was blue from boozing scotch all day.

GENTLY

Weren't you sorry for him?

FRIEDA

That's likely. I just wanted him to go.

GENTLY

And he's gone.

FRIEDA

Yes, thank Heaven. Except it's made all this trouble.

Is Miss Breske trembling a little? She is holding her hands clasped very tightly. Her eyes are lowered to the small window-table on which lie six coloured-glass paperweights. They are the right sort of paperweight, it goes without saying, but Miss Breske has surely seen them before. Yet she gazes at them now, their whorls, twists, wheels and flowers. Does Gently notice? It seems not. He smokes quietly, watches the sea.

FRIEDA

I can't help it. I'm not sorry. I won't put on an act.

GENTLY

Your mother cried.

FRIEDA

Oh, her! She would cry about anything.

GENTLY

How does Trudi take it.

FRIEDA

I haven't asked her. What does she have to worry about?

GENTLY

It doesn't seem to have affected her tennis.

FRIEDA

(Shrugs, twists her mouth.)

GENTLY

You are not very close, you and Trudi.

FRIEDA

She's the younger. She doesn't know. The war, every-thing, it was over. She doesn't remember being poor.

GENTLY

But you remember.

FRIEDA

Oh yes.

GENTLY

You wouldn't want to be poor again.

FRIEDA

That's in the past, we have money now. We work hard, but we have money.

GENTLY

And Trudi will marry some Stephen Halliday.

FRIEDA

Trudi will marry who will have her.

GENTLY

She's lucky.

FRIEDA

(Says nothing, does nothing, is still.)

GENTLY

Let's see . . . your rooms adjoin. You'll know if she was in her room Tuesday night.

FRIEDA

Will I?

GENTLY

Well?

FRIEDA

I'm not her keeper. She went to bed, that's all I know.

GENTLY

She went to bed before you.

FRIEDA

She has no responsibilities.

GENTLY

Long before?

FRIEDA

At half-past ten. Tennis makes her tired, no doubt.

GENTLY

And you?

FRIEDA

At nearly midnight, and I didn't go to kiss her goodnight. But she was in. I had locked up, and she was there in the morning.

GENTLY

You were last to bed.

FRIEDA

Yes.

GENTLY

After all the others, you alone.

FRIEDA
(Shrugs.)

GENTLY

And it was quiet.

FRIEDA

Just the sea. There's always that.

GENTLY

Yes, the sea through an open window on a warm night in July. Even there at the back you'd hear it, standing by your open window.

FRIEDA

(Stirs.)

GENTLY

Looking through the window. Across the courtyard. To the other wing. Where your mother sleeps. Was there a light?

FRIEDA

No!

GENTLY

You saw nothing?

FRIEDA

Nothing.

GENTLY

Of course, it was a dark night.

FRIEDA

I tell you, there was nothing to see!

GENTLY

But he'd be dead then, your American, smashed, bleeding, below the cliff. When you were standing at the window.

FRIEDA

No!

GENTLY

He was certainly dead by then.

FRIEDA

Oh God, I don't know anything.

GENTLY

A quiet night.

FRIEDA

I don't, I don't!

GENTLY

The sound of the sea, on a quiet night.

FRIEDA

Ask someone else – not me!

GENTLY

Who, Miss Breske?

FRIEDA

Stop going on at me! Oh . . . you make my head swim.
If I knew, wouldn't I tell you?

GENTLY

Would you?

FRIEDA

Oh, just let us alone. We didn't kill him.

GENTLY

Yet he's dead.

FRIEDA

I know, I know.

And not only dead, Miss Breske.

Frieda, Miss Breske, moans, covers her face with her hands. Gently watches the sea, the sea which is blue fire. Across the sea slowly crawling goes a white-painted trader, far out, a sea-myth, drowned and witching in the sea. And the sea spans convex, a half-moon of blue blaze. And in a straight line which is a curve goes the trader across the moon. And the moon's voice sounds along the unpersuaded shore. And Miss Breske moans, her face covered with her hands.

GENTLY

Of course, he had a secret. A very valuable secret. He was tortured for the secret. Tortured, then killed. He may have taken the secret with him or he may have given it up. But giving it or keeping it couldn't save him, he was marked for killing.

FRIEDA

That was his business, not ours!

GENTLY

He came here to be hidden.

FRIEDA

What of it?

GENTLY

Perhaps nothing. I'm trying to warn you, Miss Breske.

FRIEDA

He was a stranger, a complete stranger. He picked this hotel from the *Good Food Guide*. That's all we know of him, all we want to know. I wish to God he'd gone elsewhere.

GENTLY

(Shrugs.)

Well. But remember what happened to him.

FRIEDA

Am I likely to forget it?

GENTLY

His secret was dangerous, may be still.

FRIEDA

Oh, you just make my head swim!

Gently looks at her, she at him. Her grey eyes front his warily. Her lank hair clings to her shiny forehead. Her pallid mouth is set straight. Nothing further, Miss Breske, he says, nothing further. Now. She says nothing, rises heavily. She walks with the long stride of a man.

CHAPTER SIX

S HELTON, SQUEEZED INTO the glass-panelled office,
flanked by Sergeant Walters and Sally Dicks, the latter
a straight-mouthed, straight-haired female who, nevertheless, has some adequate measurements: Shelton has
released his seventh victim, a building contractor from
Ashton-under-Lyne: and he frowns, and thinks, and
watches Sally as Sally skims through her shorthand notes.
Shelton's thoughts are some part with the contractor,
some part with Gently, some part with Sally. The
contractor, because he was uncivil: Gently, because he
has overwhelmed Shelton. As for Sally, the heat in the
office had caused her to take off her tunic, and so to
expose, with greater definition, the generous lines of her
bosom. Shelton evaluates these automatically while more
consciously perusing his first and second subjects. He is
also aware of the contradiction between Sally's bosom
and Sally's face. Sally is grim to her neck. Sally is about
to bite someone. Her retroussé nose is needle-sharp, she
has haughty eyes and a fresh complexion. Properly, the
rest of her should be niggardly, stringy, two boards

clapped together: her face says so, is full of injury, has been struck, and would strike. Yet the rest of her is voluptuous, even muffled in a uniform. How did nature make the slip? Sally's bosom aggrieves Shelton. He snaps: You've got that down – looking for a moment as grim as she. Sally scribbles something, nods. Sally has only one expression. Then she sits straight, picks up a razor-blade, begins trimming a pencil, looking not at Shelton or Walters: in disdain of all the world. Perhaps she's queer, Shelton thinks, but takes no comfort in the thought. Meanwhile, he's let that Hutchins cheek him, which the Chief Superintendent would hardly have done . . .

Precisely then he sees the Chief Superintendent passing by in the hall. He dispatches Walters. Gently hears him, turns aside to Shelton's Aquarium. You have something? Not very much, sir (asked after like that, it seems less than nothing!) – but the last fellow, his name is Hutchins, had a conversation with the deceased. Did he, Gently says, that's progress. What did he talk to him about? About America, sir, about New York, about the real-estate racket. Hmn, Gently says, that's interesting. Yes, sir. Hutchins had been to New York. He's a building contractor in the Midlands, he had something in common with Clooney. Do you have a transcript? Gently says. I can read it back, sir, says Sally Dicks. Gently takes Sally in with a glance. Sally turns back two pages, face redder than usual. She reads, with breaks: I met him in the bar . . . Tuesday night in the bar. He was alone. I'm fresh back from the States, I asked him what part of the States he came from . . . Then, I don't know, he was in real estate, we got talking about that. They run a price-fixing

racket out there, the deceased knew the ins and outs of it
. . . names? He mentioned one I knew, a firm called
American Homes, Inc. . . . I don't know, I forget the
connection . . . No, he didn't say he worked for it . . .
Well, yes, for my money, and don't forget I've just been
over there . . . He had an accent, I don't know what, but
they're all foreigners in New York . . . look, I said I don't
know. Just an accent, right? Eyetie, Jerry, Swede, Pole,
take your pick. He wasn't Irish . . . Yes, how many more
times? He was a yank . . . he knew New York . . . knew
my hotel there was fresh-built . . . the streets, places . . .
he couldn't kid me. Then he shut up and cleared off . . .
why? Well, he just did. I didn't talk to him again . . . no,
I tell you, he seemed to avoid me. Sally Dicks stops
reading. Hmn, Gently says, yes, very interesting. It proves
a point, sir, Shelton says, now we know we're dealing
with an American. An American with an accent, Gently
says. Well, Hutchins is right about that, sir, Shelton says,
they're all sorts of nationalities in New York. You only
have to look at some of their names. Gently shrugs, says,
Well, carry on, see if you can get any more impressions.
Then he turns his broad back and walks out of the
Aquarium. Was it, after all, something that Shelton had
dug out of Hutchins? Now Shelton isn't certain. He can't
interpret that last shrug. He finds himself staring at Sally
Dick's bosom without any emotion, for or against it.

Gently continues through the hall and across the drive
and across the lawn. Trudi and Stephen Halliday are
sprawled on deck-chairs, laughing, languid, moist with
sweat. They sit in the shade of a gnarled oak tree, an oak
tree stunted by the east wind, a witch tree, with its

seaward boughs each one turned back to point landward, full of bunchy, broomy twigs and little freak pink leaves: beneath it they sit, or droop, in the deck-chairs, rackets thrown down on the short, parched turf. Trudi wears a broad blue ribbon to secure her silver-blonde hair. She has the oval family face, but it is fined and free from heaviness. It has width across the cheek-bones, a delicacy in the nostrils, a decisive line in the jaw, a lighter rounding of the chin. Also the eyes, still showing kin, have had the grey distilled out of them, are a distinct, grave blue, frank eyes, ready to smile. Trudi, surely, has inherited her portion of the Viennese fiddler's charm. The lumpish Tichtel genes have been held at bay here. Her body, too, though strong, like Frieda's, has a grace and lightness not like Frieda's, is long-limbed, poised, flexible, handsome in whole and in part, showing well now, thrown down carelessly, beside the doctor's nephew's sturdier form. By any standard, Trudi is beautiful. She has beauty that needs no bush. It needs no painting, no dressing, no calculated concealment. Let her only lie sprawled and sweating, a panting tomboy, and she is beautiful. She is beautiful, as it were, even beyond sex, to a degree (seen in actresses), suggesting sterility: as though reaching a line drawn by nature, beyond which development may not go. Frieda may have children, Trudi has her beauty. It is a means which has suffered perfection and so passed into an end. The lust which drab Frieda can stir may not readily imagine possessing her sister.

They stop laughing as Gently approaches, but don't bother to stop sprawling. Shelton, in similar circumstances, might have felt an intruder; Gently seems not to notice. He smiles, pulls up a chair, glances at the guests lounging within earshot. The guests feel an impulse to move away, and unobtrusively implement it. Miss Trudi Breske, Gently says. Trudi says coolly, Yes. Congratulations on your game, Gently says, this business hasn't put you off your stroke. Trudi quietly re-spaces her legs but doesn't feel obliged to make a comment. Why on earth should it put her off her stroke, Stephen Halliday says, Trudi is fab, nothing puts her off. Gently shrugs, says nothing. She's a right to play if she wants to, Stephen Halliday says. She needs something to take her mind off things, that's what I'd have thought. And why not tennis? Gently nods. Yes, why not? Especially with such gifts for concentration. But that's why she's so good, Stephen Halliday says, because she can empty her mind when she plays. Yes, Gently says, I was watching, I noticed. Well then, Stephen Halliday says, what's so unusual about that? Trudi is frowning, not smiling. Her frown is beautiful too. It scarcely marks her smooth forehead or produces a sensible tilt of her brows: merely grows, like grass growing, or a haze passing over the sun. I'm sorry, she says, if I enjoyed my tennis. But Mr Clooney was really nothing to us.

GENTLY

He lived seven weeks under the same roof.

TRUDI

Oh, I know, I'm sorry for him. I wouldn't want anybody to, well, die like that. But he was just a guest, you know, a complete stranger to everyone. I can't really feel about him as I would if I'd known him well.

GENTLY

He didn't play tennis.

TRUDI

Good Lord no, nothing like that. But that's not all. I mean, a lot of people don't play tennis. He was just, well, he didn't try. He didn't offer to make friends. If you said something to him it stopped there, he wasn't interested in you.

GENTLY

Not in you?

TRUDI

Oh well! There are things that men always say.

STEPHEN

They say them to Trudi, in any case.

TRUDI

One doesn't pay attention.

GENTLY

But you spoke to him.

TRUDI

I suppose so. I couldn't very well not, could I? I arrange the entertainments – games, shows, competitions. But nothing of that sort amused him. I soon gave up asking. He was – I don't know – absorbed in himself, we didn't mean anything to him.

GENTLY

We?

TRUDI

Well . . . the rest of us. We try to make people feel they belong here. The personal touch, you know? But not him. He didn't come for that.

GENTLY

No . . . did he?

TRUDI

(Looks at him quickly.)

STEPHEN

I met him too. He wasn't so bad. I'd say he was a decent sort of a cove. I got on with him all right, what few times I saw him.

GENTLY

I wonder what you talked about. You couldn't have very much in common.

STEPHEN

Oh, I don't know, one can always talk. The weather, that sort of jazz.

GENTLY

You're not in the estate business.

STEPHEN

Me? Never. I'm studying medicine.

GENTLY

You talked to him about that?

STEPHEN

No . . . once. Yes, once.

TRUDI

Stephen talks to everyone about medicine.

GENTLY

It's an honourable calling.

STEPHEN

I simply mentioned it, that's all, it just happened to come up. We were talking to him, Trudi and me. There's nothing special about that, is there?

GENTLY

(Shrugs.)

Trudi and you?

STEPHEN

Yes, for Heaven's sake, Trudi and me. What are you getting at?

TRUDI

It was really nothing. Stephen was here to play tennis.

STEPHEN

Yes, and that's how it came up. Trudi invited him to join a foursome. He said he was afraid of pulling a muscle—

TRUDI

Which gave Stephen a perfect opening.

STEPHEN

And I had a boast, that's about it. I'm an exhibitionist at the bottom of me.

GENTLY

I'd say you were doing yourself an injustice.

STEPHEN

No, not me. I'm an exhibitionist.

Gently surveys the young man mildly. Here again is a family likeness. Stephen has the same good-looking, spare features as his uncle, Doctor John. Much callower, of course, and without the sharp, cynical eyes; and Stephen is burlier, more clumsily made; but the doctor's stamp is on him. He has ceased to sprawl now, has come up straight in the deckchair. He returns Gently's gaze forcefully, is trying to stare him down.

GENTLY

What concerns me more specially is what Clooney may have said to you.

STEPHEN

The usual things.

GENTLY

Well, describe them.

STEPHEN

It wasn't anything that would help you.

TRUDI

About New York. He talked about that. How slow things seemed over here. I think he was homesick in a way, he just couldn't fit in here.

GENTLY

Why didn't he go home, then?

How should I know. He didn't tell us why not. Maybe he had some domestic trouble, you know, alimony payments. But that's guessing.

GENTLY

He mentioned his wife?

TRUDI

No. I don't remember that.

STEPHEN

They're always married, these Americans, have got a wife they're running away from.

TRUDI

Yes, he said something – what was it? About marriage out there being a bad business.

STEPHEN

You couldn't win, that's what he said. The woman had you on the hop. It sounded personal, I thought, as though he'd had some experience.

TRUDI

Yes, bitter.

STEPHEN

Bitter as hell. I wouldn't mind betting that was his trouble.

GENTLY

Hmn. You seem to have had quite a talk with him, after all.

STEPHEN

Well, I wouldn't say that. Just one thing leading to another.

GENTLY

And how did it lead to his thoughts on marriage?

STEPHEN

As a matter of fact, because of what I'd been saying. That I was studying for my M.D. He advised me to stay clear of women, not to marry till I was established.

GENTLY

Not much of a compliment to Miss Trudi.

TRUDI

Oh, he was only making fun.

GENTLY

While being bitter?

TRUDI

I – he didn't mean—

GENTLY

An interesting character, this American of yours.

STEPHEN

(Colouring.)

Just look here! We're doing our best to answer your questions. It's not as though we could tell you anything important, all this doesn't matter a rap. So at least you can stop sneering, pretending we're telling a pack of lies.

TRUDI

Stephen!

STEPHEN

I don't care, Trudi. It's like some sort of Inquisition.

TRUDI

He has to ask about Mr Clooney—

STEPHEN

Yes, but he doesn't have to be so sarcastic.

TRUDI

(Makes a little gesture.)

STEPHEN

All right, all right. You can put up with it if you like.

GENTLY

I'm quite sincere when I say he's interesting. His character seems so elusive. For instance, he scarcely spoke to other people, yet he let his hair down with you.

TRUDI

That's . . . exaggerating, perhaps.

GENTLY

Then this matter of his wife. Some people think he cared nothing about her, others that he cared very much.

STEPHEN

We said he was bitter, not that he cared.

GENTLY

I've been told he treated her as a joke. And even his physical appearance is questionable. Was he ugly – or handsome?

TRUDI

Oh – handsome.

GENTLY
(To Stephen.)
You agree?

STEPHEN
Why not? He wasn't bad-looking.

TRUDI
He was good-looking. (She blushes.) But you – you've
seen him.

GENTLY
(Shrugs.)

TRUDI
Of course . . . now, I dare say . . .

STEPHEN
He was well set-up, quite distinguished. May have had
a heart condition, but nothing exceptional for his age.

GENTLY
A heavy drinker.

TRUDI
Not heavy.

GENTLY
Drank scotch, reeked of whisky.

TRUDI
But that simply isn't true. Who has been telling you all
this?

STEPHEN

He drank a bit, like all yanks, but you never saw him the worse for it. He had a colour, I'll say that. But he never struck you as a lush.

GENTLY

Not ugly, not a drunkard, not indifferent about his wife, not even notably secretive. Well, it'll sort itself out, no doubt. Perhaps he didn't have an accent, either?

TRUDI

He was an American, you could tell that.

GENTLY

A native born and bred American.

TRUDI

I – yes, born and bred.

GENTLY

No overtones – say, Italian?

TRUDI

Good Heavens no! He was not Italian.

GENTLY

What makes you so certain?

TRUDI

He . . . it is just quite impossible.

STEPHEN

You must know that, if you've looked at him. Wrong ethnological type.

GENTLY

His name suggests an Irish ancestry. But nobody suspects him of being Irish.

No, not Irish. I'd say . . . I don't know, one only thought of him as being American. But if there was an accent . . . a slight accent . . .

GENTLY

Yes?

TRUDI

Well . . . I don't know . . . Scandinavian?

STEPHEN

Of course, yes, that would be it. You're brilliant, Trudi – that's his type exactly: a Nordic dolichocephalic.

GENTLY

You are familiar with Scandinavians, Miss Trudi?

TRUDI

I . . . a little . . .

STEPHEN

It doesn't matter. She's right, absolutely right. Ethno-logically right.

GENTLY

I wonder. As a mere layman I regarded Clooney as brachycephalous.

STEPHEN
(Staring.)

Ah, but his injury, he smashed his skull. That might give a false impression. There was a parietal collapse – Uncle John described it to me.

Oh, his skull was in a mess. But wouldn't that reduce the brachycephalic character?

STEPHEN

It might, of course – and then it might not. Depending entirely on the collapse.

TRUDI

This is silly, I know . . . but I'm not feeling too well.

STEPHEN

Trudi!

TRUDI

Sorry, Steve. It's just hearing you talk about . . .

STEPHEN

Oh hell, I should have known better.

TRUDI

I'm sorry. I'm just made that way. Just the idea gives me a turn . . . I'm a terrible coward about these things.

And certainly Trudi has turned pale, and is sitting up, and inclining her head forward. Stephen Halliday catches her hand and begins to chafe it, but she draws it away.

TRUDI

No, I'm all right, really.

STEPHEN

Damn, I'm a bloody idiot.

GENTLY

You musn't feel too strongly about Clooney, Miss Trudi.

TRUDI

(Darts him a look, says nothing.)

GENTLY

He seems to have affected people so differently, you'd think they had special points of view. Unless the difference was in him, and he deliberately gave different impressions.

TRUDI

I don't know how he affected the others.

GENTLY

Surely you know how Frieda disliked him.

TRUDI

Oh yes. But she's . . . different.

GENTLY

In what way?

TRUDI

Well . . . I don't know! Frieda isn't a happy person, she takes offence easily. She's all wrapped up in the business. That's her whole interest in life.

GENTLY

She would do a lot for the business.

TRUDI

Yes, it comes first with her.

STEPHEN

You'd have to marry it if you married her. It'd be a life sentence.

TRUDI

(A sidelong glance at Stephen.)

It's as I say, she isn't happy. I don't know what would make her happy. Perhaps nothing would. She's like that. Perhaps it's power she really wants, though I'm sure it wouldn't make her happy either.

GENTLY

She may be lonely.

TRUDI

Then it's her fault.

GENTLY

I suppose your sister was never engaged.

TRUDI

Oh, there's no great tragedy of that sort. Being jilted wouldn't squash Frieda.

GENTLY

Has she been jilted?

TRUDI

That's hardly possible, you must fall in love before you're jilted. I know it's cattish, talking like this, but I don't think Frieda could fall in love.

GENTLY

She loves the business.

TRUDI

Yes, exactly.

STEPHEN

Trudi was right about her wanting power. Her sort of love would be megalomania, she'd want a man she could put in a cage.

GENTLY

But then, if she lost him—

STEPHEN

She'd be dangerous. She wouldn't shed any tears.

GENTLY

You seem to have studied her case, Mr Halliday.

STEPHEN

Well, yes, psychology is part of my job.

GENTLY

Then perhaps you can tell me – a trained observer – what offence Clooney gave to Miss Breske.

STEPHEN

He didn't jilt her, I can tell you that.

GENTLY

But, you would say, he was some threat to her power?

Stephen Halliday stares silently a moment. Trudi sits hugging her brown knees. Trudi has not quite regained her colour, she may be encouraging its return by keeping her head low. The position, however, exhibits her fine shoulders, and the tanned grace of her back, and the regular spacing of strong vertebrae receding handsomely to the dress-line. You cannot discompose Trudi into anything short of beauty.

STEPHEN

It's a theory, of course. But I don't see how it's possible. If you mean Clooney was making up to Mrs Breske, I can only say that no one noticed it.

GENTLY

No one?

STEPHEN

Well, generally speaking.

TRUDI

I say the idea is ridiculous. I would have noticed—

GENTLY

Yes?

TRUDI

But I didn't. No, there's nothing in it at all.

GENTLY

Yet the news of his death upset your mother.

TRUDI

Of course, she's hysterical, she enjoys a scene. She'd storm and howl over a flat soufflé, let alone a guest being killed. That's her way.

GENTLY

So Frieda told me. Yet your mother is a shrewd woman.

TRUDI

Oh yes.

GENTLY

Too shrewd, I'd have thought, to enjoy a scene in front of the guests. Were you present, by the way?

TRUDI

I? – no, I slept through it.

GENTLY

(Raises his eyebrows.)

TRUDI

I can't help it! I just did, that's all.

GENTLY

So you're not a witness to how your mother reacted.

TRUDI

No, but I know how it would be, mother going off the deep end, Frieda being wildly efficient. But there's nothing in it, nothing at all. It's simply what you'd expect. He didn't mean anything to mother. You're quite wrong about that.

GENTLY

Then perhaps to Frieda he meant something.

TRUDI

Frieda? Oh, that's absurd!

GENTLY

Why so, Miss Trudi?

TRUDI

Can you imagine it, a man like that, and Frieda?

(Shrugs.)

I'm afraid I can. It doesn't seem a bit improbable. A man of fifty, perhaps not a strong character, might easily become infatuated with your sister.

TRUDI

Oh, that's likely. You don't know Frieda, she doesn't invite infatuations. Besides . . .

GENTLY

You were saying?

TRUDI

It's completely impossible, absolutely. It couldn't be.

GENTLY

Completely impossible.

TRUDI

Yes, yes.

GENTLY

I wonder how you can be so certain.

TRUDI

(Is her colour fading again?)

I just know. I know it.

GENTLY

Yes, there's one way you could know it.

Trudi hugs her knees very tightly and stares over them at the fawn turf. If no blue ribbon were containing her hair it would be drooped forward about her face, but there is a blue ribbon, and her face is naked, and it is as pale as it has ever been.

STEPHEN
(Angrily.)
I think that stinks! I think that's a wicked thing to insinuate.

GENTLY
What, Mr Halliday?

STEPHEN
That he – that fellow – should have been carrying on with Trudi.

GENTLY
Carrying on?

STEPHEN
Yes, carrying on – that's what you had in mind, wasn't it? So then she'd know it wasn't with Frieda, that's the 'one way' she could be certain. Oh, very clever!

GENTLY
You interest me.

STEPHEN
Yes, and I can see what it's leading up to. You're trying to put me in the middle, aren't you – finding a fat motive for me.

GENTLY
You seem to have found one for yourself.

STEPHEN

Go on, go on. Say I killed him.

GENTLY

Is this a confession?

STEPHEN

You'd like that, wouldn't you?

GENTLY

Psychology is part of my job, too.

STEPHEN

A *crime passionel* – how convenient. Clooney slain by jealous lover. Crazy medical student slices victim before hurling him over cliff. I fit the part, oh beautifully! A manic depressive, why not? You can tie that label on to anyone, they don't need any spots.

GENTLY

Where were you that evening, by the way?

STEPHEN

Oh here. Right here. I don't have an alibi worth tuppence, I'm your man on the spot.

GENTLY

Visiting Trudi?

STEPHEN

Spying on her. Creeping around in the bushes. My crazy jealousy on the boil, a case of lancets in my pocket. Then I saw – does it matter what? When a man's in that state it scarcely matters. But something snapped in my

98

unbalanced mind, and I followed my victim to the cliffs. Just ask my uncle. He knows I was out, knows I came back at the critical time.

TRUDI
(Dully.)

There's another way.

STEPHEN

Oh, don't go spoiling it.

TRUDI

My room . . . it's next door to Frieda's. If she . . .

STEPHEN

The Superintendent will hate you.

TRUDI

Well, I'd know. That's all. Not the other . . . not that.

STEPHEN

For shame! You've made it completely commonplace.

TRUDI

Anything like that . . . it just isn't.

She tosses her head back, as though now willing to let her face be seen, but her eyes are still lidded low, her linked fingers dragging together.

GENTLY

Are you so certain you'd know, Miss Trudi.

TRUDI

Yes. Yes, I'm certain.

GENTLY

When you're such a sound sleeper.

TRUDI

(A faint flush.)

You must believe me.

GENTLY

(Shrugs.)

Not that it matters whether he slept with her or not. He may have tried and been repulsed. Or she may have visited his room.

TRUDI

No!

STEPHEN

You see? Frieda is snow-white, Superintendent.

GENTLY

(Nods.)

Yes, I see. Anything like that just isn't. And strangely enough, I'm inclined to believe it.

STEPHEN

Crazy. Now I shan't confess.

He glances at Trudi, but her eyes are closed, are hidden entirely by bluish lids.

CHAPTER SEVEN

T HE AQUARIUM, WHICH was never intended for long sittings, is getting unbearable to Inspector Shelton, who may not stand the door ajar and has only a twist ventilator to bring him air. There is a fan, a small fan, its boss as large as its blades, but its only function, other than an introverted hissing, is to redistribute a fixed humidity. Shelton has tried switching it off. Then the humidity seems to congeal. He has tried facing it in a variety of directions, but each seems less efficient than the last. Short of taking the roof off, Shelton feels, nothing will make the Aquarium tolerable, and the impossibility of this perfect solution hangs heavy on his soul. He sets fire to a limp cigarette, directs a puff of rank smoke over Sally Dicks's head. Sally Dicks ignores him. Shelton closes his eyes. If ever, he says, if ever, if ever. Talk about routine, Sergeant Walters says. I could weep, Shelton says, I bloody well could. Because what are we doing? We're doing sweet Fanny Adams. Not a blind bloody bit of this matters a puke. Just going through the motions, that's what we're doing, like checking a perm without any draws. He knows, we know, none of these sons of bitches are suspects, they're as pure as the driven slush, they just come in here to cheek us. I suppose someone has to do it, Sergeant Walters says, just our rotten bad luck it was you and me. If ever, Shelton says, there's another case of murder I'll resign and open a clip joint. This isn't police work, not the way I know it. It's bloody murder. It's death to policemen. Watch it, Sergeant Walters says, there's his royal highness coming over.

Gently comes in, glances round him. They could swear he knows what they've been saying. It seems printed on the air in a number of balloons which he is reading off in those glances. What's the tally, he says. Eighteen, Shelton says. You'd better have a break, Gently says. Miss Dicks, get them to send in a pot of coffee. Oh, and Miss Dicks, leave the door open. It's like a steam-bath in here. Miss Dicks smiles, or moves her face, and goes out, leaving Shelton staring after her wonderingly. Hah, Gently says, and sits down in the chair vacated by Sally Dicks. And suddenly, strangely, there does seem a meaning in the grinding statement-taking of Shelton and Walters. Gently's presence gives it a meaning, throws over it a glamour, a promise of fertility. Among those statements, it now seems almost certain, lie precious grains of the first significance. Tell me, Gently says, has anyone noticed if Clooney ever visited, say, Mrs Breske's parlour? – when immediately, standing out like an Epstein sculpture, an enormous fact takes substance amongst the rubbish. Yes, he did. Two people have mentioned it, a Mrs Piper and a Mr Wade: a Mrs Piper from Weston, near Bath, and a Mr Wade from Higham Ferrers. What day was that? On two separate days, Friday of last week, Monday of this, two visits, each in the afternoon, though of duration unknown. Mrs Piper saw him tap at the door, heard Mrs Breske's scolding Herein! Mr Wade saw him leaving by that door a short while before afternoon tea. That was the fact, ending there, exciting nobody's special curiosity, since guests often visited Mrs Breske's parlour to admire the bric-à-brac and furniture. Outside which, Gently says, nobody noticed any particular relations between Clooney and the Breskes? Wait, yes, Shelton says, afire with enthusiasm, several of them noticed he had an eye for Miss Trudi. Of course, she's a doll, all the men . . . but he often passed the time of day with her. She's the one he talked to most, more than to anyone else. More than to Frieda, Gently says. To Frieda or Mrs Breske, Shelton says, nobody has him talking to Frieda, you get the impression they weren't pally. Any other impression, Gently says. Shelton shrugs, says, mostly negative. But sure as Christmas he didn't talk much, which makes it stand out he talked to Trudi. Well, Gently says, well. Shelton squeezes his brain for more matter. Tell me, Gently says, you've checked the staff here, the male staff: there are seven, aren't there? Seven, Shelton affirms, or eight including the gardener. But seven live in? Six: the kitchen boy comes from the village. And they are the two chefs and the four waiters? Shelton opens his notebook, says, Yes: Lehrer and Kaufmann, the assistant chefs, the waiters Klapper, Gordini, Dorfmann and Friml. They are regular staff, Gently says. Yes, Shelton says modestly, I did check. They've all been here since Easter at least. Gordini and Friml were here last season. Hmn, Gently says, it was a man who killed Clooney, a man who wanted something from him, a man who knew Clooney had something to give, a man who knew more of Clooney than we do. Otherwise, I'd have said . . . Shelton drinks it in greedily. At last, a glimpse of the great man's thinking, after questions all the morning! That's why he was killed, Shelton says, because he had something the other man wanted. Hmn, Gently says, that's basic, it wasn't mere revenge, or to stop Clooney's mouth. But what did Clooney have? Money! Gently smiles at sweating Shelton. If money, how was it known he had it, except by knowing where it was? And if one knew where it was, one could steal it without murdering Clooney: then it was a question of, in his absence, simply collecting it from the hiding-place. But, Shelton says, inspiration firing, suppose it was someone from Clooney's past, knowing from past events that he had the money, but not where he had hidden it since he came here. Illegally obtained money, of course, Gently says. Of course, Shelton says, that follows. Hmn, Gently says, but then why kill him, either if he tells or if he doesn't? One way you commit a superfluous crime, the other you lose the secret for ever. If the money is illegal you can let him live, he can't come to us with a complaint. But are killers logical? Shelton urges. Gently smiles again, says, Perhaps, in this case. It may be that Clooney was doubly vulnerable, having both dangerous money and dangerous knowledge. Shelton grapples with this complex notion, asks, What sort of dangerous knowledge? Or, Gently says, just the dangerous knowledge which, admitted under torture, made his killing certain. As for example a knowledge of the identity of a person who dare not own to that identity. But what – who – ? Shelton gapes. The Breskes have Jewish blood, Gently says. They were refugees from Hitler's Austria. Mrs Breske had a Nazi, presumably Aryan, uncle, who seized her sister's estate after the annexation. All of which may mean nothing or everything, as far as our present knowledge goes. Shelton stares at this amazing man, who can produce, so casually, such a shaft of illumination. He opens his mouth, and closes his mouth, his mind reeling in turmoil. And Clooney, he gulps, Clooney was the uncle? It makes a certain sense, Gently says. Who knows – knew – something about someone, like Eichmann – that sort of thing? Shelton gabbles. Less inconsistencies, Gently says, as, why the Breskes harboured him in the first place. Shelton is silent. He is overwhelmed. He has never before met this level of intelligence. He feels like a child with a hideous algebraic problem, whose despair is resolved by the huge wisdom of an adult. He had no key, it was impossible; the key is provided, all is plain. At a single blow Gently has smashed the impasse, shown how the terms fall into place. All, that Shelton had stared at so hard, is suddenly, without violence, coherent and related. I looked over both his rooms, Gently says, the one he had first and the other. Shelton gazes at him uncomprehendingly, knows nothing about Clooney's rooms. No signs of tampering, Gently says, though of course, the searcher may have had a key. And no place, I'd say, to hide anything, no loose boards or panels. So either he was criminally careless (the smile is deep in Gently's eyes) or he hid the money elsewhere, where, conceivably, it still remains. Shelton finds Gently looking at him, as though expecting comment. Money, Shelton says hoarsely, what money? The suppositious money, Gently says. But there won't be any money, Shelton exclaims, they didn't kill the uncle for money! Gently's brows lift fractionally, the faintest sketch of elevation, but it is enough, it demolishes Shelton: he collapses in awareness of his crass density. We know nothing of that, Gently says, it's simply one of several hypotheses. I've asked for information about Mrs Breske's uncle and talked to U.S. Security about him. If he's Clooney we shall hear, but till then we let him ride. On the whole it is probably not too likely that Clooney was Mrs Breske's Nazi uncle. But ... it's such a wonderful angle, poor Shelton says. The uncle, Gently says, was only a minor criminal. He served a sentence. We shall probably find him occupying a respectable government post in Vienna. Shelton shakes his head limply, his xs and ys dancing again, and is only saved from saying something truly stupid by the return of Sally Dicks with a pot of coffee.

They drink the excellent Viennese coffee and Gently lights his pipe and blows smoke-rings. The famous pipe, Shelton notices, is a straight sandblast, and is filled with a mixture of modest price. Later on the great man will switch to a cut plug even more modestly priced, but after eating, after coffee, he entertains his palate with the milder plant. Sergeant Walters is also a pipe-smoker but he has a fancy pipe with an aluminium stem. He feels the inferiority of this weapon and puffs nervously and aside. Gently, alight and surrounded by rings, is a spectacle of grandeur not rashly to be challenged, and Walters knows it, and offers no challenge. He is a lesser man. He smokes scented flake. Sally Dicks, a clean-living non-smoker, almost purrs in the presence of Gently smoking, which Shelton feels to be unfair (though entirely in character with Sally Dicks), while Shelton himself sucks a casteless fag, the low limit, and subsists.

Well, Gently says, having drunk his coffee, have you had statements from the waiters? Befagged Shelton coughs, says hastily, Not yet, though I've talked to them of course. And it happens again: he has an irresistible persuasion that high significance is resting here, and that the waiters, far from being mere routine, are really what the case is about. I thought I'd have them in next, he adds apologetically, I thought I'd wait till you were here too. Oh, just go ahead, Gently says, I shan't have much to ask them myself. Which conjures up for Shelton a terrible picture of himself mishandling this very rich material while the great man watches and blows rings to his gallery of Walters and Sally Dicks. He says fiercely to Sally, Go and get hold of one of them. Which one sir? Sally asks. The nearest one, Shelton says, I'm not particular (trying to sound like a man who can make grist of anything). Sally goes and returns with Friml, surely the least promising of the quartet: a withered and resigned man of fifty who looks pathetic in baggy *Lederhosen*. Johann Friml? Yes, is me, sir. Take that chair, will you Friml? Friml sits with a curious caution, as though expecting his nobbly knees to creak. He has a narrow, grey, fleshless face with deep straight lines at each side of his mouth and small faded grey eyes and a pendulous nose and invisible lips. Friml would never have looked young and at fifty

Friml looks very old. If there is sense in Friml, you begin to think, it would extend no further than to picking a loser. Shelton goes about him cannily, remembering the Wicked Uncle in the background. Name, age, profession, birthplace (pause); Where were you in the war, Friml? Friml peers at Shelton palely. In the war? That's what I said. Friml shrugs wanly. I am in Vienna, I work in the cafés, oh, the shortages, the American bombers . . . Were you a party member? Friml is perplexed. A party, yes? Is it the union? No, Shelton says, not the union, the Nazi Party, were you a member? Friml gives a sort of choking chuckle and his eyes twinkle at Shelton: as though Shelton, in his British innocence, had tumbled on some incommunicable national joke. It makes Friml jolly in his misty way. He cannot share it, but he cannot resist it. He wags his head from side to side and his invisible mouth works and creases. Well, Shelton says, were you or weren't you? I am a waiter only, Friml tries to explain. So? So, what use would they have for Johann Friml, who moreover has only one lung, and arthritic joints? Just answer the question, Shelton raps. Friml repeats his choking chuckle. No, no. No, no. This angry Englander must see it is funny. Shelton glares and does not see it, but he can get nothing more positive out of Friml. The more Shelton tries, the more Friml chuckles, till moisture trickles from his merry eyes. Well, answer this, Shelton thunders, you were in Vienna under the Nazis: did you know a certain Gauleiter Tichtel, a relative of your present employer? Gauleiter Tichtel? Friml wipes his eyes. Yes, once, certainly, he knew a Tichtel, a Walter Tichtel, that was his name, he worked as a soap-boiler in

108

Salzburg. Walter Tichtel. It brings back memories. Friml remembers him quite plainly. He married a chambermaid called Herta Schnitzen and went to live at Klagenfurt . . . A Gauleiter Tichtel! Shelton bawls. Friml shakes his head: not this one, no. He was a soap-boiler, that is quite sure, and his wife was a Schnitzen from Wiener Neustadt . . . And there is much more about the Salzburg soap-boiler which now comes trippingly to Friml's mind, so that if an entry: Tichtel, W. (soap-boiler), had been required for a National Biography, Friml, at this happy moment, could have supplied it extempore. Shelton stares venom at the waiter. By now he knows he'll make nothing of Friml. The man is a fool, he is beyond interrogation, his mind has no straw with which to begin. Idiocy and wisdom alike are the foils of inquisition. Shelton draws breath. Never mind, he says, never mind about soap-boilers and chambermaids, let's hear what you know about Wilbur Clooney and what you were up to on the night he died. And so they bumble and fumble through Friml's statement of which the best part, after all, was probably his reminiscences of W. Tichtel.

Rudi Dorfmann comes next and makes better carving for savage Shelton. Rudi, blushing and plump, in all things Fool Friml's antithesis. Rudi is bright. He is Mrs Breske's favourite, acknowledged to be more than a drudging servitor, is, in fact, an apprentice caterer from a good Hochstadt-bei-Zoom family. Mrs Breske is acquainted with that family and has been entrusted with Rudi's education – in the catering line, though Frau Dorfmann has not excluded more general departments of knowledge. Rudi has a future. Rudi at last will be model hotelier. You may trace it already in his intelligence and his smiles and his comfortable build. Twenty years on Rudi will meet you at the door of a recommended hotel and his smile and embonpoint will assure you immediately that comfort and attention must be yours. He has the knack and instinct of hospitality. Only, just now he is a little shy with it. Just now he blushes and his brown eyes roll and his Cupid's lips tremble and stammer. He wants to please you, wants to please Shelton, and above all, Herr Inspektor, but he is aware, and his blushes stem from it, that as yet he doesn't quite know what will please. Sit down, Dorfmann, Shelton says. Rudi jams his tight trousers into a chair. He has a broad, moist face with a button nose and fine light brown hair that disarrays romantically. The hair is disarrayed at present and a lock lies limply across his forehead. He rolls his eyes at Sally Dicks who stares waspishly then turns to her pad. Shelton hurries through the preliminaries. Rudi is earnest in his replies. He speaks in hasty but good English and in a voice that sounds as though it broke but lately. Good, Shelton says, good, and stares at Rudi for some long seconds, at the end of which Rudi is very red and smiling all round the Aquarium. So where were you when it happened? Shelton says gruffly, his voice vibrant with disbelief. I, Rudi says, I, I, I am in bed, yes, I believe. How do you know that? Shelton says. I, I don't know it, Rudi gasps. Then why do you say it? Shelton asks. I, I, Rudi says, it is just what I think. We don't care what you think, Shelton says, we can do our own thinking, Dorfmann. What we want from you is the truth, and the truth we are going to have. Now start again. And in this way Shelton bullies and browbeats unhappy Rudi, whose only desire, did Shelton but know it, is to please Shelton in all things. But alas, Shelton cannot be pleased. Rudi is transparently an innocent. He knows nothing that can be of service to Shelton in the mystic progress of his wrath. He splutters and stammers and blushes and writhes and pummels his mind for minute details, for the telling trifle, the key to it all, the one phrase that will delight. No good. He fails utterly. His angry customer remains angry. A lonely spark, good for a minute, is all the light he can stumble upon. Shelton says, He drank plenty, didn't he? – referring of course to X(Clooney). I, yes, it is so, Rudi gulps, he had an arrangement with Mrs Breske. An arrangement? Yes, it is arranged. How arranged? demands Shelton. I do not know, I, I, I am told of this, I do not know. Mrs Breske told you they had an arrangement? Naturally, yes, Mrs Breske. Something like he didn't pay for his drinks? Yes, that is so, he does not pay for them. But you chalked them up to his room number? I, no, is not required. But you chalked them up? Rudi shakes his head. He sort of drank on the house? Rudi nods. Well, well, Shelton says, glancing at Gently, and then he does it, he actually smiles, and Rudi blushes in sheer relief at this tiny frank of his honest endeavour. From the molten slag-heaps of Shelton's ire he has picked a rose, just one.

So his drinks were free, Shelton says to Gently, after Rudi has blushed his way out of the Aquarium, well, that's an arrangement I'd like to have somewhere with a cellar as good as Edith Breske's. It may have been a genuine arrangement, Gently says, with Clooney staying here *en pension*. She'd know within a little what his drink bill would come to so she could add a margin and make a flat charge. Did you ever hear of it being done? Shelton inquires. I don't stop much in Hotel Continentals, Gently says, but I dare say if we question Mrs Breske she will have this explanation ready for us. Shelton gives Gently a look. I'd say it's more like he's one of the family, he says. The harder you look at this so-called Clooney the less he adds up to being a guest. Gently nods, says, Yes, a strange guest, but still not behaving like one of the family; much more like a fugitive, Gently says, though from what remains open. A fugitive being sheltered by Mrs Breske, Shelton says. Gently nods again, says, Let's have Gordini.

Gordini comes. He is Mrs Breske's taste, and Sally Dicks views him with interest. He is not exactly the taste of Sally Dicks, but Sally allows he might be acquired. For Carlo is mightily, southernly handsome. His Austrian garb sits splendid upon him. He has shoulders, and knees, and hands, and a nape, and hips, and a chest, and black curling hair. He has a statuesque neck that moulds and ripples and a head that sits heroically upon it and his swarthy skin is goldeny swarth and his black eyes smoulder on a trigger. He has a Grecian nose of surprising straightness that ends in a tip of blunt power, a full-lipped mouth, incandescent teeth, a smooth, rounded, dictatorial chin. So handsome is Carlo, Mrs Breske's taste, that one could forgive him for a trace of swagger, but swagger he has not, he is quiet and obsequious, very parfait, very serviceable. Only that glitter in Carlo's eyes suggests that Carlo is ever otherwise. Sally sees it, or rather feels it, and shivers, and sulkily sharpens one of her pencils. The play begins. Carlo sits. He sits grandly with parted knees. He too speaks English with a quick fluency and in a pleasant pure baritone. He is from Milan? Well, no, Milan is not his home town, he comes from a village near Marsala, but where, of course, there is no work. He has worked in Naples and Ventimiglia, then for five years in Milan. So he's a Sicilian? Carlo shows his teeth. But nobody can make a living down there. His family, man, they are so poor, they would catch a cat and boil it for dinner. Carlo sends them a small allowance without which they would starve. He visits them. They are so thin. They live on a spaghetti that scours them like pigs. Here Gently clears his throat and asks a question: When was Carlo in America? Carlo swivels his head on his magnificent neck to face Gently, says, Never at all. Where, then, did you learn English? Carlo laughs with all his teeth. Man, all the Italians speak yankee English, how else would the tourists understand them? You learned yours from tourists? Gently asks. Partly from the tourists, Carlo says, but in the first place from Giovanni, Giovanni Montelli, who is a cousin who has emigrated. Giovanni is rich, Carlo says wistfully, America is a wonderful place for a Sicilian, he comes back to the village like a millionaire, man, that wad of notes he has in his pocket. Why haven't you joined him in America? Gently asks. Carlo shrugs, says, Some-day, maybe. But I am just a poor peasant boy and Giovanni is someone else again. What sort of someone? Gently asks. Carlo shows his teeth, says, You wouldn't understand, man. To understand you have to be born there. Just say Giovanni had some influence. And that influence helped him in America? You may say that, yes, Carlo replies. It is all tied up, this side, that side, the right people go over there and make good. It's not just money, you understand, but whatever it is, Carlo doesn't have it. Though Carlo is lucky, too, in his way, he is earning big money by the standards of San Antioco. You see Giovanni often? Gently asks. Carlo shakes his head. It was but that one time. Giovanni had come back, like most successful Sicilians, to show his fine clothes in his native village. He had bought a villa for Uncle Pietro and a vineyard to go with it, and he had taught Carlo some waiter's English and paid his fare to Naples. It was enough. He had behaved handsomely. He had set Carlo free from his prison of poverty. Carlo speaks his name, Giovanni, with reverence, as of a noble thing, a strength, an inspiration. And Gently asks no more about America or Giovanni but lets Shelton proceed on the old worn trail. The dead man, Clooney, Shelton resumes, what can you tell us about him, Gordini? Gordini can tell them very little that they haven't heard ten times already. Was he an American? He speaks like one, but man, his accent was terrible. He wasn't Italian? Shelton has to be joking. In Gordini's opinion, Clooney was German. German or Austrian? Shelton demands. German or Austrian, he could be either. What did Mrs Breske think he was? Gordini looks angry, says she never spoke of him. Not even to you? Shelton says unbelievingly. Gordini looks daggers and won't answer. Shelton likes this and keeps needling him, Shelton is adroit at using the needle, he stabs Gordini through detail after detail of the evening and night of Clooney's dying. But perhaps he is wasting his talent after all, though he stabs out every fact he goes for, because he is shutting Carlo up like a night-safe and getting just and only what he demands. He has offended Carlo. Carlo is proud. He is not a swaggerer, but he is proud. And at last even Shelton begins to realize that he may be mishandling a useful card. Look, Gordini, he says, you don't have to fight us, we're not trying to hang something on you, all we want is to get at the facts, for chrissake give us co-operation. But now it's too late. Carlo is shut up, sitting straight and splay-kneed, chin at an angle, not like, as he claims to be, a peasant boy, but more like a grandee suffering affront. An interesting character, this Gordini. Sally Dicks thinks so, whatever her taste.

He goes. Shelton lights a cigarette. He is only too conscious of having fumbled that one: he searches his brain for some twist, some gimmick to raise his stock a little with Gently. Suppose, he says, Gordini's lying, and Mrs Breske, she's lying – collusion, in fact – a mutual alibi – giving Gordini opportunity ... Miss Breske would need to be in it too, Gently says, if Gordini was not to be locked out of the hotel. I'd say that checked pretty well, Shelton said, I don't trust that girl further than I could throw her. Yes, it adds up, a little family conspiracy, with the Eyetie lover as hatchet-man. He'd probably do anything for Mrs Breske – and every Eyetie can use a knife. But what was it about? Gently says. Shelton hisses smoke, says, Does it matter? If he's a Nazi uncle with a nasty secret or some other chiseller trying it on? It'd still be nice to know, Gently says, especially as we don't have any, what you might call, proof. Yeah, Shelton says, hissing still, but it's a nice idea. I like the idea. And he frowns profoundly over his idea as though he, if not

Gently, can appreciate its significance, as if he sees a hundred subtle correspondences, each worth a tumbril-load of proof. No Eyetie lover-boy with curls can make a monkey of English Shelton. Fetch Klapper in, he says suddenly, ringingly, in a tone that proclaims his mind is made up.

Klapper comes then behind, fourth and lastly, Franz Klapper, from Ischl he, town whose name alone is affront sufficient to tease Shelton: one does not find a vowel supporting such a train of consonants in countries respectably placed with Greenwich. But Klapper, coming last, and it appears grudgingly, has a quality denied to his predecessors, namely that he alone, like the grass growing, wears and ornaments his national dress. It sits upon him. He is born to it. Not the alpenhorn outside is more truly Austrian. Aryan Franz, blond, loose-limbed, gentian-eyed, fair-cheeked, strong of bone, springy of step, he walks in off the mountains. He is Austria: you could engrave him for a stamp or a coin, set him to music for a national song, carve him in stone for a monument. He is sifting snow and spring blossom and heroism and a waltz and the sleeping valleys and the gay towns and the mirror lakes and the white sun. That is, until he opens his mouth. Then Shelton pins him in a moment. It needs not Gently's delicate ear to assess the origin of Klapper's English. Where, Shelton demands, did you learn English? And Klapper is suitably, encouragingly, confused. He moves his square shoulders awkwardly and would rather not understand Shelton. But he does understand him, so at last he says, Sure, when I was in the States. So you've been in the States? Shelton purrs. Yes, Klapper was over there for a while. Doing his job there are chances for travel, and Klapper enjoys seeing the world. When were you there? Shelton says softly. For the last two years, until January. Then Klapper felt restless for a breath of Europe and he came first to London, afterwards here. Two years, Shelton says, making it sound damnatory, and certainly Klapper takes his meaning: if a sojourn in the States is not precisely criminal, still, it can be to nobody's credit. And you were in one place? Shelton murmurs. Yes, no, that is to say, in several situations, as, a season at the Waldorf-Astoria, then other places, that is usual. But in one town? Yes, in one town. Which was? Klapper babbles it out: New York. New York, Shelton smiles, isn't that a coincidence, Clooney coming from New York and all? Why, Shelton says, reducing New York to the size, if he knew it, of barbaric Ischl, you probably ran across him while you were over there, in a couple of years you'd meet lots of people. Did you meet him? Klapper wants to escape, his eyes dart this side and that of Shelton. Did you? Shelton repeats, in a wild surmise. And Klapper, in a panic, blurts out ... Yes! Yes! It explodes among them! It explodes in Shelton! He can scarcely speak! Not daring to look at Gently, he sits crouching, hearing triumphal music on the hills. Yes, Klapper said, Yes, in answer to Shelton's question, Yes, as a result of Shelton's technique and Shelton's handling, Yes, he'd said, Yes, Yes. No statesmen, labouring to gain approval at a convocation of all nations, wrought from Russia that sacred word with such brave joy as Shelton now knew. Well, well, he says, when he can say anything, well, Klapper, well, well, and looks almost lovingly at Aryan Franz, who, notwithstanding, seems far from well. But fancy, Shelton continues, fancy your not telling us you were acquainted with the late Clooney, especially, Shelton says, when we've been breaking our necks two days trying to find out who in hell he was – that, Shelton says, wasn't very nice, Klapper, not, as we say, very co-operative, in fact, Shelton says, we may throw the bloody book at you, just for that if for no other – and, Shelton says, you can put your shammy trousers on it, if there is some other, we shall find it. Then he breathes in and out with great ferocity, and Austria wilts before the man. Now, Shelton says, who was he? But sir, I don't know! Klapper exclaims. If I knew anything I would tell you, sir, I sure would, I want to co-operate. Yes, it looks so like it, Shelton says. Where did you meet him? What was he doing? Sir, Klapper says, he was only a customer, I just don't know anything about him at all. He comes, he and one or two others, to the restaurant I work at for a while – that is Cassidy's, off Fifth Avenue – a few times he comes there. And you wait on him, talk to him, Shelton says. No sir, no, Klapper says, they never sit at my table, I never spoke to him at all. There are three, four of them come in together, one is an Irishman called Pat, one is a little dark man called Toni, then there is Mr Clooney, who they call Heifiz. Who they call what? Shelton yaps. Klapper winces, says, Heifiz, sir. That surely is what it sounds like, though Klapper didn't pay much attention. Heifiz, or Heifitz, the *z* German. Or possibly Heifetz, Gently suggests. Or possibly Heifetz, Klapper allows, willing to keep the matter open. Heifiz, Heifitz or Heifetz is how the others referred to Clooney, while they ate and drank, not inexpensively, in a toney joint off Fifth Avenue. And that was his first name, Shelton pursues. Klapper thinks no, sir, it was just a nickname, as for instance the fourth man, in appearance Armenian, was always referred to as Abdul: Pat, Toni, Heifiz and Abdul, they were all nicknames, Klapper opines. So what sort of people were they? What sort? Did they seem like honest citizens? Klapper wrestles with this one, says, It sure is difficult, I never could tell with Americans. They dress and act, you know? – without taste, without manners. Maybe you're talking to a millionaire, maybe a hoodlum fresh out of Sing-Sing. Unless you're born there, Klapper thinks, you goddam cannot tell the difference, and with regard to Pat, Toni, Heifiz and Abdul, he would not like to venture an opinion: except they were noisy, rather ugly men, who it would have been no pleasure for Klapper to have served. But you served Clooney here, Shelton snaps, how come you said nothing to him about having seen him before. Sir, he is a stranger, Klapper shrugs, I had no desire to be familiar with him. But you said nothing to anybody, Shelton snaps. Nobody has said to us, Klapper knows him. What was all the mystery about? Sir, he just meant nothing to me, Klapper says. He wriggles his shoulders and then explains: I sure didn't want to get mixed up in this. I didn't have anything important to tell you, sir, and I thought you would certainly know all about him. It's just I've seen him before, nothing else. I don't know anything about who killed him. And neither does he, for all Shelton can extract in half an hour of sinewy question: he finishes up where he began with those shadowy figures dining in Cassidy's. Pat, Toni, Heifiz and Abdul, a brood of mixed nationalities, foreign to Klapper, who actually saw them, and hopelessly foreign to Shelton, who didn't: foreign and worse, because over the rawness, the primary colour of their alienship, was scumbled this secondary glaze of Americanization, levelling, greying-out, rendering shapeless. Wouldn't it have been better, after all, if Shelton had failed to uncover this tantalizing glimpse, which leaves Clooney, Wilbur or Heifiz, even more enigmatic than before? Pat, Toni, Heifiz and Abdul. They dance like motes before Shelton's eyes. He has got them, but doesn't know what to do with them. Or maybe they have got him.

CHAPTER EIGHT

A FTER LUNCH THE Great Man is to be seen on the
cliffs, wandering lonely there, if not like a cloud, at
least like some roving demi-god. The reporters mark him;
they would wander with him if they could overcome
their shyness, in the manner of disciples following a
peripatetic philosopher, to grave his words upon their
memory. But shy they are, or perhaps unchosen. They
wander apart, below on the beach. He wanders above,
aloof, unchallenged, his words unspoken and so un-
graved. What does he know, moving so slowly in the
fire-blue sky, hidden now by scenting gorse, now
marching large on stony hillock, along the crumbling
cliffs northward, while all the larks sing? He has been
telephoning, this is known, and the calls were trunk calls.
To Whitehall? To Grosvenor Square? Rumour stays not
the question. But there was matter worth transmitting,
and this surely irks the reporters, so that, though shy, still
they will not let the Great Man from their sight, and
follow, from the common sands, his heavenly motions
aloft, his slow, sightless, mindless motions, informed,

heavy with news. He has it, they are certain, what they can print in explosive type in the late editions, and they may not, cannot, and on all counts will not, let this seminal figure stray from view.

He wanders, and above the pill-box stops to take a bearing. He looks outwards into a jewel of arching sky and splendid sea. The sun twinkles in a corner and floods the jewel with far blaze and shows illimitably blues strained with gold grey and green. And pressing behind him like firm hands is the gorsey heat of the cliff-top within which the larksong, a trembling spirit, wreathes, to be felt more than heard. And centrally in that jewel (because thus he has placed it, where the heel of the compass ethereally sweeping from north to south shall rest) lies the concrete lump, tilted and burying, hooking its rusty claws savagely, exposing broken surfaces, weathering but obdurate, and moulded surfaces, their purpose lost. All below him lies that lump and in the lump Stody's theorem. The lump, descended thunderously, had blundered clear of the still-scarred cliff. You cannot drop a pebble on it. You must needs throw the pebble. Neither can you drop a body on it. You must needs throw the body. Throw a body? The theorem requires it: must be thrown to reach the lump: must be picked up, or, if alive, grappled with, and thrown or hurled, say, three yards. A notable feat on a dark night! Yet the theorem requires it. Clooney limp or Clooney kicking, he would need to be heaved three yards. Had Clooney then been inflated with hydrogen? Or was his heaver no mortal man? Had the Devil himself descended on Clooney and whirled him, with supernatural precision, thence? The

Great Man perhaps considers the Devil along with another dozen surmises, which cannot help including Brother Fred's concept of a walking, running or leaping American; for the Great Man and Brother Fred are one in seeing clearly what is set before them, and, while not entirely discounting the Devil, alike prefer the obvious answer. A leaping American? With limbs whirling, furiously from the dewy brow, in perfect darkness, or near enough, towards the invisibly murmuring and spreading sea: frantic to do, yet coolly accurate to choose his spot within feet, sans marker, sans light, sans any view of the lump below. Did he do it by the stars, this leaping marvel, astrally guiding himself to oblivion? The Great Man retires with measuring steps. He halts but five strides from the brow. He sees now below the dejected reporters and the combers washing, but the lump he does not see. And where it is below the mute cliff-line stretches faceless and unbroken, grassed thinly, a smooth extension offering direction to no man. Even in the staring light of noonday, how could Clooney have hit that bugger head-on? Or less than the Devil, who could have heaved him so irresistibly and correctly? Yet, with the coin suspended, one remembers again the bruises and the twenty-two cuts, and the obvious, about to proclaim itself roundly, retires a little, still to wait. A mystery here! Not what was done, but how in the Devil it could be doing.

The Great Man's figure shrinks further but does not wholly disappear, and the watchers, kicking the dried bladder-wrack, know he ponders the spot where the hat was found. Stody has marked this spot: at first with a twig, but later with a finely-fashioned stake: it stands boldly beside a gorse-thicket and bears his signature in indelible pencil. The spot is pleasant. It is a sort of haven protected by the thicket from the sea-breeze, an odorous sun-trap, inviting for lovers, exquisite for picnics and such traffic. The breeze sifts among the gorse and stirs the sweetness of ten thousand blooms, each straining its yellow hood in the high heat of afternoon. What terror of death could harbour here? Only Stody's stake insists on it. The dried grass meekly refuses to bear evidence in support. Here was the hat, Stody insists, inferring, Here Clooney was thrown down and tortured, but the spot, speaking in its own language, allows this assertion no reality, saying instead, These things are pictures less in truth than a humming bee. Two kinds of reality? Ah, but, define the term. If Clooney's agony is unreal then no bee hums. All is real or none is real or all and none are real/unreal: make-believe is come again, and that's an attitude, mark. The spot and Clooney, raw essence, equally turn their backs on labels. They are modes of feeling, to use words. We, not they, contradict. But here this Man selects his mode, though aware of its illusory character, and while not preferring it to other modes, which he acknowledges, yet pursues it with single mind: among the gorse, with bees humming, he insists with Stody on Clooney dead. And what sees he, pursuing his mode? Nothing more revealing than the stake. There is nothing to see, not the ghost of a print, not a shred of material caught in the gorse. Stody has been here many times, Shelton, Williams have both been here, the reporters, to a man, have gleaned on their heels, spurred on by fame to make discoveries. But the hat was all, and the position of the hat, and the fact that the hat was lying on its crown: was, was here, and was thus, period, is the whole story. Why then does the Man stand so long and so dreaming at the spot? What new intelligence has he brought, to extract fresh matter from the gorses?

He comes out of this dream. Another approaches him. The reporters are alert and apprehensive. Has one of them, less shy than his fellows, braved the Great Man's displeasure? But no, the newcomer is quickly recognized: is Stephen Halliday, the doctor's nephew: their ruffled feathers sleek again and they fall into surmising. Stephen Halliday ranks not over-high in their private list of hot suspects. They watch him, seeing his mouth move, but hearing naught save the fret of the sea. I wanted to talk to you alone, Stephen Halliday is saying, facing Gently across the stake, there may be nothing in what I have to tell you, and it's rather embarrassing to tell you at all. Is it to do with Clooney? Gently says. Stephen says, Well, it's up to Gently to decide, it's, in a way, a psychological matter, but, really, he thinks he ought to mention it. Right, carry on then, Gently says, and Stephen Halliday makes as though he will; but instead, for some moments, he stares at the stake, though all the while speech is straining at this throat. Then he comes out with it, saying, It's Frieda, saying it in a forced, low tone, as one might admit to some embarrassing disorder which may no longer be concealed. And he lets it hang there, the bare name, as though merely to mention it tells all, and Gently, being cognizant of the concept, Frieda, can flesh the bones without further prompting. And Gently can, so it seems, for he makes no reply. With Stephen Halliday he silently considers the name thus sounded, like a key in music. Frieda, Miss Breske, sullen Frieda: like thunder rolling on the cliff-top, a black cloud, muting the larks, sealing the scent in the blooms of the gorse. It may be nothing, Stephen says, but already he has made it too much. By speaking the name, and in that tone, he has given the matter a violent twist. He has moved it bodily. It will never again return to its aspect of a moment before. He has turned it a little into the light and the light can never now be dispelled. And he is too conscious of having done this, standing there, his eyes on the stake, conscious and confounded that through him, and so simply, the revolution has taken place. He did not mean it. He was adding a little, a very little to Gently's stock: then that little was suddenly much and an avalanche descending. He had snapped his fingers and brought the roof down.

GENTLY

When was this?

STEPHEN

Oh . . . more than a year ago. I hadn't met Trudi, you understand. Trudi was away at a school in Hertfordshire. Trudi's a good deal younger than Frieda.

GENTLY

Tell me about it.

STEPHEN

I simply met her, you know how it is. I was down from Edinburgh on the long vac and mother, uncle, we all dined here. Uncle knows the Breskes of course, a G.P.

knows everyone. So we had our coffee in the parlour along with all the gash furniture.

GENTLY

How far did it go?

STEPHEN

Oh, hell . . . all the way, I suppose. Frieda has no morals, you know: none. She just hasn't developed a moral sense.

GENTLY

And this went on till you met Trudi?

STEPHEN

You make it sound so damned odious. But it wasn't like that. Frieda wasn't in love with me, it wasn't a question of love between us.

GENTLY

What was it a question of, then?

STEPHEN

Of, of sex, I suppose you'd say. She made a point of letting me know she was willing, and, of course, I was; so that was that. I mean, when you're my age you *want* sex. It's a hellish great thing and you want to know about it. Women gnaw at you, all women. Any woman will do. It isn't love.

GENTLY

And with her it was the same.

STEPHEN

I don't say that. Not quite the same. It isn't the same with women, you know. Sex is always a means with them.

127

She taught you that?

STEPHEN

Now you come to mention it. Yes, that's something I learned from her. Before then it didn't really come home to me, perhaps I didn't want to believe it. You like to think . . . oh, I don't know! Of course, I'm as romantic as hell. I'd like to think women come to it on the same footing though of course they don't. Perhaps not even Trudi.

GENTLY

And what was sex a means to with Frieda.

STEPHEN

Oh, power. That's her god.

GENTLY

She wanted you to marry her?

STEPHEN

That was her target. God help me if I'd ever fallen for that.

GENTLY

You were never actually engaged.

STEPHEN

No. My Scots canniness saw me through. I think people like Frieda always overreach themselves unless they're dealing with positive fools. She tried the old pregnancy trick, you know? Imagine that − with a medical student! I offered to do the tests myself, and of course she had to cry off. God she was furious.

GENTLY

I can well imagine it.

STEPHEN

She's rather frightening when she's angry. Doesn't get
hysterical, doesn't shout. It just burns away inside her.

GENTLY

When was this incident, Mr Halliday?

STEPHEN

At the end of the long vac. Now I think of it, just
before Trudi came home – yes, it was. Just before.

GENTLY

And when Trudi came home . . . ?

STEPHEN

Look, that was the end of it, that business about the
pregnancy. Frieda knew she'd shot her bolt, there were
no more get-togethers after that.

GENTLY

Frieda quietly faded out.

STEPHEN

Yes – no. In effect, yes. If you'll only listen to me—

GENTLY

You may be sure I'm listening.

STEPHEN

Well, that's entirely what I've come to tell you.

And once more Stephen hesitates, as though again
weighed down by a word of thunder, such a word as,

when spoken, may chain-react to infinity. He stares aslant
at the thicket gorse of the tender pod and nesting spines,
the spicy gorse, always glad, where (X) Clooney's hat has
rested.

STEPHEN

Actually, it could have been quite innocent. I mean,
one is apt to imagine things.

GENTLY

What sort of things, Mr Halliday?

STEPHEN

About people's motives, of course. For instance, you
see a man looking into a car and at once you think he's a
thief, but he may be only the owner of a similar car, or
perhaps he's considering buying that model.

GENTLY

You caught Frieda looking into a car?

STEPHEN

Not exactly into a car. They had some rats under the
floor in a storeroom. She asked me to get her something
to poison them.

GENTLY

After . . . Trudi came home.

STEPHEN

(Nods.)

GENTLY

And you suspected a connection.

STEPHEN

Yes, I did. Don't ask me why. I thought she was aiming to do us in.

GENTLY

Trudi and you.

STEPHEN

Yes.

GENTLY

Well, your uneasiness is understandable. Did you give her the poison?

STEPHEN

Not bloody likely. And she didn't ask for it again, then.

GENTLY

(Looks inquiringly.)

STEPHEN

Oh yes. She had another try three weeks ago. And the rats are there, that's a fact, because she took me in and showed me. So I gave her some sodium bic crystals done up in a jar labelled arsenic, and presumably they did a good job, because I've heard no complaints.

GENTLY

You think she used them?

STEPHEN

(Shrugs.)

Anyway, that's what I had to say. Maybe it's a lot of damned nonsense on my part, but I felt it ought to go on the record.

GENTLY

Why, Mr Halliday?

STEPHEN

Why? Because I'm afraid of her, that's why.

GENTLY

You afraid of her?

STEPHEN

Because of Trudi! Frieda hates her, don't you see?

Does Gently see? His eyes rest on Stephen with no particular focus, so that he seems rather to be listening to some far-off sound than to be hearing Stephen's words. Is it the cries of children below, or the piping scold of sea-swallows? Or is he so far beyond and behind those words that his hand is on the root to which they are the flower? Perhaps after all his eyes are seeing, through Stephen, whole tapestries of deed and secret enactment. Why? he says. Why?

STEPHEN

But I've just told you why!

GENTLY

Why should Frieda be dangerous to Trudi now? Isn't that what you're asking me to assume?

STEPHEN

Yes, but—

GENTLY

No. Listen to me. It's over a year since you met Trudi. During that year Frieda is apparently resigned to Trudi's

132

taking you from her. If there is anything in this notion of yours that Frieda had murderous intent, then plainly she gave up the idea when you refused to supply her with rat-poison. But now you say she's at it again. So why? What's happened to stir her up afresh?

STEPHEN

How should I know—

GENTLY

Who would know better? You are in Miss Trudi's confidence.

STEPHEN

But damn it, it might be something Trudi didn't know about. There's no knowing the way Frieda's mind works—

GENTLY

No, Mr Halliday. It is something you know about. You are so certain the threat is to Trudi. A new element has come into her relationship with Frieda, and recently. What?

STEPHEN

I just don't know!

GENTLY

Oh, Mr Halliday. It was Clooney, wasn't it?

STEPHEN

I tell you—

Don't bother to protest what isn't true. The facts are really self-evident. Clooney was living here off the Breskes. They supplied him with pocket-money and board. It follows he had some hold over them, was privy to something to their prejudice. And he was friendly with Trudi but not with Frieda. There's no point in denying any of this.

STEPHEN

You'll say next that Frieda killed him—

GENTLY

Of course. You take the words out of my mouth. I am not likely to believe Frieda would want to poison her sister when Clooney presented such an obvious target. And when the sodium bic made no impression she turned to other, surer means. But she couldn't have killed him herself. Who can we implicate along with her?

STEPHEN

You – you're taking the mickey now.

GENTLY

Am I going too far?

STEPHEN

You don't believe me, do you? You think I'm just trying to shop Frieda.

GENTLY

I certainly do think that. And then I ask myself the reason. And I remember that Mr Halliday has no alibi, and that his interest is tied up with Trudi Breske's.

STEPHEN

Oh my God!

GENTLY

For example, if Clooney is planning to squeeze the Breskes dry, then it is going to make a difference to what Trudi Breske brings to her future husband.

STEPHEN

You don't – *believe* what you're saying!

GENTLY

Why not? People kill for less.

STEPHEN

But good God man, I wouldn't! Can you see me as a killer?

GENTLY

That's stuff for the jury. I deal in facts. Just now you're placed rather queerly, Mr Halliday. If you do know what hold Clooney had on the Breskes this would be a good time to tell me.

STEPHEN

But it can have nothing to do with, with the other.

GENTLY

Let me judge.

STEPHEN

No! I tell you . . .

He hangs his head and tells Gently nothing, that is to say, in words. But who can ever tell nothing to this luminous-eyed, omniscient man? He knows too much. All combinations, all permutations of the facts are simultaneously present and under review in the quiet laboratory of his brain. Give him a word, and it fits. Give him a silence, it fits no less. Everything is there Advance or withdraw, you cannot escape from his net. Stephen Halliday, sinewily intelligent, with the spiritual toughness of a born surgeon, is lost, and knows he's lost, and feels humility and strange admiration. Danger he doesn't feel. He knows he's innocent. And that too Gently is fully aware of.

GENTLY

So why don't you tell me.

STEPHEN

I can't. It's a matter of loyalty, that's all. If I knew anything about who killed him, do you think I wouldn't tell you?

GENTLY

Your loyalty doesn't extend to Frieda.

STEPHEN

Because, damn you, I'm scared of what she might do. I *am* scared. I can't protect Trudi. And Frieda is kinked. You must know that.

GENTLY

Frieda must have a cogent reason . . .

STEPHEN

All right, all right, that's understood. For a person like Frieda, a cogent reason. A reason like people have killed for less.

GENTLY

Which you're not going to tell me.

STEPHEN

No. I promised. And it doesn't matter. Because you know. You've asked the right questions and got the right answers and the proof is probably on the way. And if I can guess that, then Frieda can guess it, and if she's going to act . . . don't you see?

GENTLY

I see you have a melodramatic turn, Mr Halliday.

STEPHEN

God, you've got to take this seriously!

GENTLY

Poor Frieda. She works so hard.

STEPHEN

(Stares at Gently. Says nothing.)

CHAPTER NINE

Had gently asked the right questions? Certainly a right answer, or nearly a right answer, came tripping that moment across the Atlantic – bounced off Telstar, to be decoded and dispatched by one Cy, Cyrus Fleischer. Shelton received it, Walters next had it, Stody conveyed it to the cliff-top. Is Clooney listed as a missing person? Gently had asked; and Stody is able to pant, Yes.

Yes: at least, a certain Albrecht Stenke has been so listed by New York Police, and Stenke matches at all points the description of (X) Clooney. He is aged fifty-two, same height, same colouring, very similar in feature, is of German origin, lived in the Bronx, was clerk in a real-estate company, American Homes, Inc. Furthermore, Stenke is married, though living apart from his wife (an explosive Polish lady who runs a cheap lodging-house in the Lower Bay dock area); he is addicted to scotch (says his landlady) and kinda dresses smart (same authority); and he quietly vanished from his usual haunts on or around 10 May. A match, a palpable match: for (X) Clooney read Albrecht Stenke. New York Police have Stenke's fingerprints and shortly will put the matter beyond doubt. (X) Clooney has been dragged back from his anonymity, the chill void that settled round him: New York Police have pinned him down, given him habitation, a name.

But – and this is the uneasy feeling that comes to Shelton after the first fizz has settled, and before the Great Man enters with Stody running before – has pinning (X) Clooney down really got them anywhere, with respect to throwing some light on his latter end, or has it merely given substance to the speculations which their previous research seemed to justify? There is so little fresh in this information! The name is changed, but what's in a name? For the rest, the New York Police, in explaining Clooney, seem almost bent on explaining him away. He has no record, they say, no known criminal associates (they are apparently oblivious of that sinister trio, Pat, Toni and Abdul); he was solvent, had no worries, was generally liked, possessed friends; in fact, was knocking along through the world as well as most and better than many. They do not know why he vamoosed. He was a least-likely in that respect. They had checked with friends, firm, wife and not come up with a single clue. One day, 10 May, when it had not been even raining, this rather likeable clerk had packed a bag, cleaned out his account, and blown. It happened all the time, sure, but you could mostly put your finger on something, while with this character, nix, he seemed to have done it out of pure cussedness. Stenke had no relatives, the report says, he was admitted as a refugee in 1946. He worked as a labourer, as a waiter, as a musician, as a storekeeper, married Lydia Brodetsky, 1953, joined American Homes,

Inc., 1955. All of which, though rounding the picture, suggests no great leap forward to Shelton.

So much the more surprising, then, that the Great Man, carrying this report in his hand (and waving it, as a cabinet minister stepping out of 10 Downing Street might wave some document fraught with a nation's joy, for the benefit of the reporters – and the reporters mob him with fizzing cameras) assumes, as he sails through their ranks, an expression, a twinkling eye of satisfaction, as though that report in his hand were the necessary key to the entire corpus of the mystery. He comes into the Aquarium and slams the door on the uproar of reporters. You've read it, of course? he says to Shelton. Yes, Shelton admits, I glanced through it. Get me the American Embassy, Gently says. We've nearly sewn this up, Inspector. All we need now is a line on those men who Klapper saw Stenke with in the restaurant. Pat, Toni and Abdul! So they were, they did come into it! But how, where had Gently connected them – what divine frisk had his intellect taken? Shelton gets the Embassy, gets Fleischer. Gently talks, states his requirement. They'll surely do that for him, Fleischer replies, yessir, back home they were probably on to it already. Especially the associates of these men I wish to know, Gently says, and if they are part of an organization, the names of the top men. No trouble at all sir, Fleischer assures him, the B'reau will certainly have that information. Oh and details of any job they may have pulled, Gently says, on or around 10 May.

He rings off, sticks his pipe in his mouth, sucks some air through it happily. Shelton stares, Sally Dicks's bosom heaves, Walters jiffies, Stody stands. What we need to do now, Gently says round his pipe, is to clear up the collateral circumstances at this end. Then, when the Americans send us that information, the decks will be clear and we can move. There are still two possibilities here and we must take care to eliminate one of them. I think that now we should have no difficulty in precisely establishing the deceased's identity. The dabs will do that for us, sir, Shelton says, relieved to find himself in routine country. The dabs? Gently says, looking mildly at Shelton – so mildly that Shelton at once begins to colour and stammer. The dabs, sir – they'll tell us whether Clooney was Stenke. I think that's fairly certain, Gently says. But it will tie it up, settle it, Shelton stammers. I sincerely hope so, Gently says. Is Shelton really so abysmally stupid as he feels at this moment? Without doubt he has missed again some refined nuance of Gently's thinking. It is important, must be important, that (X) Clooney is proved to be Stenke – and yet, the mat is pulled from under Shelton when he dares to assent to this point. Gently takes pity. We do not know who Stenke is, he says. And the pinch is that Shelton himself had begun to think along these lines! But Shelton had stopped short. He had merely said to himself, What's in a name? Nothing, of course: but behind every name is an identity. He – he was a refugee, Shelton babbles. Just so, Gently nods. A German refugee admitted into the States after the war. Under the name of Stenke, which might have been Schmidt or possibly Schultz or Schickelgruber. The Nazi uncle! Shelton exclaims. That, Gently says, we must now establish.

He glances speculatively around the Aquarium, which

Shelton half-expects to offer information, then shakes his head, says, Not quite the setting we require. Setting for what? Does the Great Man intend to raise spirit messengers – perhaps the ghost of (X) Clooney himself, for a session of immaculate inquiry? But no – Ask Mrs Breske to step this way, he says to Stody, and she, least spectral of mortals, comes scowling in, floury of hand. I wish to talk to you and your daughters, Gently says. Is not convenient, spits Mrs Breske. I think it had better be convenient, Gently says. I could of course request your presence at Police Headquarters. But I baking am, Mrs Breske spits, I cannot spare myself from the kitchen – and Frieda is preparing afternoon teas – and Trudi you will not soon find. Notwithstanding, Gently says, I wish to see the three of you in five minutes, and also, because this office is small and not entirely private I suggest we have our talk in your parlour. Mrs Breske's eyes pop, swell spitefully, but audibly she gives only her nasal buzz – though repeated three times, with a snatching of her head. Constable Stody will look for Trudi, Gently says, you will bring Frieda. In five minutes. Mrs Breske flings her squat body round and stumps out, scattering flour.

So, according to fiat, they gather in that sea-watching room, where the exquisite huntsmen and their exquisite horses gambol over floor and furniture: Mrs Breske, no longer floury, but scowling still at all and nothing; Frieda, her daughter, lumpish Frieda, drab-faced, flat-faced, grey eyes neutral; and Trudi last, heavenly Trudi, Vienna's, Austria's, wonderful child, with some mischievous, delightful exploit only now fading from her smile. Mrs Breske marches to the rocking-chair, sits, is angry with it

142

for rocking. Frieda makes the effort of going to a chair in the most distant and shadowy corner of all. Trudi sinks, sits, reclines, part-Recamier, part-tennis-girl, on that gilded, eighteenth-century sofa which must have cost Mrs Breske so dear. The others, Shelton, Walters, Dicks, melt variously into a room now growing small: Stody guards the door without: Gently sets his chair in the centre.

GENTLY
(Exhibiting Fleischer's report.)

I am happy to be able to tell you we have succeeded in identifying your late guest. His real name appears to have been Albrecht Stenke and he was resident in New York. He was a refugee of German origin who was admitted to United States citizenship. He has one next-of-kin, a Polish lady, whom he married after the war.

Gently pauses, as though for reply, though in fact he has asked no question. He looks from Mrs Breske to Trudi, then through the shades to faceless Frieda. Mrs Breske breathes thick through her nose, Trudi drops her eyes before Gently's. Frieda you would say was sitting very stiffly but you cannot quite make her out in her corner.

GENTLY

Stenke was living apart from Mrs Stenke and he was employed by a real-estate agency. He disappeared on 10 May and was the subject of a Missing Persons inquiry. The New York Police were unable to find him or discover any reason why he should disappear. According to your register he arrived in this hotel, as from London, on 24 May. (He gazes at the ceiling for a moment, the ceiling which is garnished with plaster fruit, then says, softly, as though with only personal curiosity), But why? Why come here?

MRS BRESKE
(Agitatedly.)
Ach, Gott, why does anybody come here? The food, the wine, the music – we are everywhere in the books!

GENTLY
You have many guests from New York?

MRS BRESKE
Ach – so – from all places!

GENTLY
Can you name just one?

MRS BRESKE
There will be in the register—

GENTLY
We have checked your registers.

MRS BRESKE
(Buzzes.)

GENTLY
Perhaps Miss Frieda can explain this oddity? Because really it does seem to need explaining. Not many clerks suddenly vanish in New York to reappear in an East Coast hotel. In London, perhaps, you might find such a fugitive,

or in one of the large towns in the north. But at Mrs Breske's Hotel Continental! How can we believe it was accidental?

FRIEDA

He said he found our name in a guide.

GENTLY

No doubt he did. But why choose it?

FRIEDA

He was a German. What is there surprising about him choosing our hotel?

GENTLY

(Producing a book from his pocket.)

Here's a copy of that guide. It lists over three hundred hotels and restaurants run by Austrians or Germans. Nearly a third of them are in London. There are half a dozen along the coast. Two are within ten miles of your own. Why did Stenke come here?

FRIEDA

All right, then – it's a mystery!

GENTLY

Surely not, Miss Frieda. There is such an obvious reason why Stenke came here.

MRS BRESKE

Ja, he is bad luck, that is why – always, for ever, he is bad luck!

You make my point, Mrs Breske. He came here because he knew you.

FRIEDA

No!

GENTLY

Is it worth denying, in the face of fact and probability?

FRIEDA

You can't prove it.

GENTLY

I think I may. And in the meantime, I intend to assume it.

FRIEDA

It is a lie, we did not know him – never, never! – till he came here!

GENTLY

But he knew you, Miss Frieda. That is what I am saying.

And this so strangely silences Frieda, who goes quite still in her shadows, though puzzled Shelton, who hangs on the phrase, cannot detect its sharp significance. Nor only Frieda: the open mouth of Mrs Breske declares her cognizance, while Trudi's neck is beginning to mantle, her firm, fair fingers to pluck at her sleeve.

GENTLY

Stenke once worked as a musician. And he had a nickname. Heifetz.

MRS BRESKE

He did not ever work here, not if he is called Paganini.

GENTLY

Paganini?

MRS BRESKE

Or Fritz Kreisler. A violinist is what I mean.

GENTLY

Who said Stenke was a violinist?

MRS BRESKE

Ach, did you not tell me they call him Heifetz?

GENTLY

But he was a violinist?

MRS BRESKE

How should I know what he is, that fellow? I do not talk to him, do not question him – he is another guest, you understand—

GENTLY

But surely you talked to him when he visited this room?

MRS BRESKE

Ach, Gott, who has been saying anything of the sort!

GENTLY

We have statements to the effect that he visited you, at least twice.

MRS BRESKE

This is lying – is not true—!

GENTLY

I don't think our informants lied. I think Stenke – the violinist – the refugee – visited your room more than twice.

MRS BRESKE

No!

GENTLY

Why not? He was here a long time. You are in the habit of showing guests your furniture. And your photographs – wouldn't they interest this refugee, this – Viennese, was he? – this violinist?

FRIEDA

And if he did visit my mother, what has that to do with anything?

GENTLY

Surely a great deal, Miss Frieda. It shows a considerable measure of acquaintance.

FRIEDA

Are you saying because of that she killed him? Went out and pushed him over the cliff?

GENTLY

Is that your theory?

FRIEDA

I – no!

GENTLY

Of course, we have to consider everything.

MRS BRESKE

I do not know – about my photographs – this is nonsense, all nonsense! So it is he comes here – all right! – still, I do not speak a lot to him.

GENTLY

Yet he must have had so much to tell you. So long it was since you'd met.

MRS BRESKE

But I tell you—!

GENTLY

All the war years, before, after: Vienna, Berlin, New York.

MRS BRESKE
(Makes her buzzing noise.)

GENTLY

And the Polish lady, did he mention her – what was her name . . . Lydia Brodetsky? Perhaps you had a laugh over that? Told this Stenke he hadn't changed?

TRUDI
(Jumping up.)
I've had enough! Can't you see he knows everything, mother? Oh my goodness, what's the use of sitting there and letting him humiliate you?

FRIEDA
(Jumping up too and coming to confront her.)
Keep your mouth shut, you by-blow!

TRUDI

I won't – it's too fantastic! There's just no point in keeping quiet.

FRIEDA

You'll shut up—

GENTLY

Stand back, Miss Frieda.

MRS BRESKE

Ach, mein Gott – I'm going mad!

TRUDI

You're all so blind, that's the trouble. And you think that other people are blind too.

FRIEDA

If you say a word—

TRUDI

But he *knows*! He's simply squeezing you to make you confess. And I know too – all, everything – so who do you think you're fooling?

FRIEDA

You know nothing!

TRUDI

Yes – he told me!

MRS BRESKE

Mein Kind—

TRUDI

Oh mother, what's the use? I've known for weeks now, and I don't care – it doesn't matter to me a bit.

MRS BRESKE

It . . . does not matter?

TRUDI

No. None of it. I think it has all worked out for the best. I wanted to tell you that, Mütterlein, I wanted you to know it was all right.

MRS BRESKE

Trudi, Trudi . . . ach, Trudi!

TRUDI

I don't want anything to change. Nothing between us, Mütterlein. Everything to go on as before.

MRS BRESKE
(Weeps.)

TRUDI
(Goes to her, puts her arm round her).
Mütterlein, Mütterlein. When were you not the best of mothers to me?

MRS BRESKE
(Weeping.)
Ich bin schlecht, ich bin schlecht!

TRUDI

No, don't say that, Mütterlein.

MRS BRESKE

Ach, how could you forgive me?

TRUDI

There is nothing to forgive, Mütterlein, nothing.

FRIEDA

(Stares murderously at Trudi, her blunt fingers hooking at air.)

GENTLY

(To Walters.)

Fetch that photograph which stands on the what-not.

(Walters hands it to him. Gently studies it, then glances at Trudi.)

You are not Mrs Breske's daughter, of course.

TRUDI

No.

GENTLY

In effect your real name is Trudi Lindemann.

TRUDI

I am Mütterlein's niece. I am the daughter of her sister, Mitzi Lindemann.

GENTLY

But you were brought up to think you were Trudi Breske.

TRUDI

Yes. I didn't know who I was till recently. I knew I was like that photograph, naturally, but that sort of thing can happen in families.

GENTLY

Who told you different?

TRUDI

Uncle Martin.

GENTLY

By whom you mean the deceased.

TRUDI

Yes. He knew all about what happened in Vienna. He thought I should know who I was. I never knew my parents, of course, but Uncle Martin told me about them. My father was Professor of Music at the University . . . I believe he was a distinguished man. My mother's health was never very good and she died soon after I was born. Just before that my father had been arrested. Nobody knows what happened to him.

GENTLY

Then, apparently, you were registered as the daughter of your aunt.

TRUDI

That was necessary, don't you see? Mütterlein had a permit to leave the country, but she could never have got one for me.

MRS BRESKE

Dass ist wahr, mein Gott! Without this she is finished. I promise Mitzi when she is dying – swear I take her baby with me. Ach, that journey! With Frieda two, and Trudi crying – crying – crying. What do you know about this? What do the English know about anything?

GENTLY

And Trudi Lindemann remained Trudi Breske.

But yes – how can it be different? How do I know the English will take her if she is not what the papers say? Und when she grows up, shall I tell her then all the terrible things that happen – how her father is put into an Ofen, how her mother is dying of grief? Nein, nein! Better she think the ugly old woman is her Mütterlein, that she haf a scamp for her father – ach, yes! Much betterer!

TRUDI

Oh mother, mother, you're *not* ugly.

GENTLY

But after the war, when the Nazis were beaten, when the estate of your sister was properly administered . . . was it so much better then?

MRS BRESKE

It is the same. How can I show that Trudi Breske is Trudi Lindemann?

GENTLY

Perhaps you couldn't. But you inherited the estate and had it in your power to gift it to your niece.

MRS BRESKE

She is then a child still!

GENTLY

But not now. When did Miss Trudi become twenty-one?

FRIEDA

(Fiercely.)

What does that matter? Did she make all this – our hotel, our business? Oh no – oh no! It was mother and I who did that. It was we who worked sixteen hours a day, seven days every week – while Trudi lived like a lady: first at school, then here!

TRUDI

But Frieda, I wouldn't dream—

FRIEDA

What right has she – tell me that? It was mother who gave her life in the first place: Trudi Lindemann wouldn't be alive today. And if mother hadn't risked her own life then – if she'd left dear Trudi to the Nazis – there wouldn't have been any question, would there, about who Aunt Mitzi's money belonged to. No, no! When she became a Breske she gave up her rights as a Lindemann. She was equal with me then and she is equal with me now.

GENTLY

The law views it a little differently.

FRIEDA

Where was the law in Hitler's Vienna?

GENTLY

Your mother did a brave thing, but that doesn't make a wrong a right.

155

MRS BRESKE

I do not wrong her! Ach, the money is now four times, five times – she will have more, much more, than poor Mitzi is leaving her.

GENTLY

That may be so, yet still a wrong has been committed against her. I imagine the courts' decision will be that this hotel belongs to Miss Trudi.

FRIEDA

Never!

GENTLY

Oh, I think so.

FRIEDA

We'll pay her out, and no more.

GENTLY

But you were in illegal possession of the principal, so you will scarcely be allowed to retain the increment.

FRIEDA

(Thrusting her face towards his.)

This is our work – we made it! Nobody is going to take it away. I'd sooner burn the place to ashes than hand it over to her.

GENTLY

You'll fight, will you?

FRIEDA

Yes – fight!

To establish your illegal possession?

This place is ours!

What a pity, Miss Frieda, *that your father knew different.*

Snap! The trap has closed, and Frieda is suddenly, shockedly aware of it. Her pale-lipped mouth is caught open, her next retort stopped in her throat. Her wolfish eyes have grown wild, protruding, echoing Mrs Breske's and her flat, kitchen-pale cheeks have turned a new, floury, grey. Her breath won't come. She stares and stares. Gently watches, casual, expressionless. Mrs Breske, mouth open too, drags at her daughter with her eyes. Trudi's eyes are incredulous, Shelton's baffled, but drinking it in: Walters, who knows his place, glances furtively, as though not wishing to be thought to interfere. Only Sally Dicks, that model stenographer, relishes that moment only with her ears, her pencil, one of several waiting, poised, alert for the next syllable.

Let me recapitulate the situation. Mrs Breske inherits her sister's money. She – and you, Miss Frieda – are both aware that the money properly belongs to Miss Trudi. Miss Trudi however does not know she is the daughter of Mrs Lindemann, and the only person who can possibly tell her has vanished into wartime Germany. Miss Trudi does not and cannot know. It is safe to proceed on that basis. So Mrs Breske invests the money in this hotel, and with the especial aid of Miss Frieda, makes it prosper.

MRS BRESKE

Ach, yes, is true – Frieda works so hard.

GENTLY

That was my impression, Mrs Breske.

MRS BRESKE

The books, the staff – she is good. I cannot do it without Frieda.

GENTLY

Nevertheless, all this prosperity – of which you, Miss Frieda, were a principal agent – arose from the misappropriation of the Lindemann estate. It was balanced on that. If a whisper of Miss Trudi's origin ever reached her, then the Hotel Continental, representing years of effort, would be lost – if nothing worse.

MRS BRESKE

How . . . worse?

GENTLY

An offence was committed. You cannot be unaware of that. Certainly Miss Frieda is not so unintelligent as not to know an offence was involved. The loss of the hotel and perhaps prison were the penalties of Miss Trudi finding out, and any prospect of this happening would be a very serious threat.

TRUDI

But it wasn't – isn't! You must listen to me – I would never have done such a thing to mother!

Perhaps not, but your mother and sister couldn't be certain of that.

TRUDI

Yes they could – they know me! Mütterlein, you know me, don't you?

MRS BRESKE

Ja, ja.

TRUDI

Frieda?

FRIEDA

(Shrugs.)

TRUDI

You see? They knew I wouldn't behave so. It is true what Frieda says – so true! – that Trudi Lindemann wouldn't be alive. I am here because I became a Breske, because Mütterlein took me for her daughter. And there cannot be two standards, one for then, one for now. Mütterlein has the rights of a mother with me, and I am glad, proud to be Frieda's sister.

FRIEDA

No sister of mine.

TRUDI

Yes – sister! Equal with you, the way you said. If you don't love me, Frieda, I'm sorry.

MRS BRESKE

Ach, ach, is Friedachen's way.

But I'm afraid the facts of the matter make all this irrelevant, Miss Trudi. It is self-evident that your mother and sister didn't trust you enough to confide in you. There can be no two ways about this, they either trusted you or distrusted you; and plainly they distrusted you. They intended to keep you in ignorance of the deceased's identity.

FRIEDA

So we did. What then? What reason had I to trust this *sister*?

TRUDI

Oh, Frieda!

FRIEDA

Oh, Trudi! Aren't we the sweet little miss? But not so sweet, not so sisterly when it comes to other people's fiances. You soon had your hooks in Stephen Halliday when you came tripping back from college.

TRUDI

I didn't know—

FRIEDA

You didn't want to! You just reached out and grabbed him. Not that I care – if he's such a fool you can have him and welcome. But trust you? Schweinefleisch! I wouldn't trust you to carry out the swill. No, I wouldn't have told you who was staying here – what was my father to you?

GENTLY

In fact he represented that threat I spoke of.

FRIEDA

Yes – another worthless person! He came running to us . . . never mind that. I don't care what you think.

GENTLY

He came running to you when he was in trouble?

FRIEDA

Oh no, you can't put words in my mouth. He was in England, he found us up – reckoned we would be a soft touch.

GENTLY

Which you seem to have been.

FRIEDA

Not me. I would never have let him in the house. He was trouble. I knew he would talk to her, even though he promised not to. But mother let him in – she's soft, a hard-luck story always gets round her – and we were stuck with him. If this hadn't happened he'd have been here for life.

MRS BRESKE

Frieda, Liebling – he was your father!

FRIEDA

And a drunken sponger – you know it! Living like a guest, stuffing, boozing – even his pocket-money came from you.

MRS BRESKE

He is my husband, once, once.

FRIEDA

Yes – half-a-hundred women ago.

Ach, do not speak so. Poor Martin! Perhaps I wronged him after all.

And as she weeps a few fat tears, gross, suety Mrs Breske, dragging across her eyes thick fingers, on one of which the gold still glimmers, mourning, it maybe, not (X) Clooney, not Albrecht Stenke, nor Martin Breske, but a memory of that Vienna when the world was young and gay, when Strauss, lilting from a young man's fiddle, lifted her heart among the nightingales, and the Danube, blue, forever blue, flashed, flowed along with the voice of spring. What will fetch such tears from Frieda, when she sits as her mother now?

GENTLY

Why did he come to you, Mrs Breske?

MRS BRESKE

(Shrugging.)

Who can say? He is in trouble, that is certain, and Martin never had any money.

GENTLY

Did he speak of this trouble?

MRS BRESKE

He says he wishes to lie low where he cannot be found. He is afraid that someone will come. We change his room so he can watch the gates.

GENTLY

Was it the police he feared?

162

MRS BRESKE

Ach no. I ask him this at the first.

GENTLY

Did he name, describe anyone?

MRS BRESKE

No. He says he does not know who will come.

GENTLY

But he must have hinted at the nature, the source of his fear?

MRS BRESKE

(Shaking her head.)

Nothings. I think it is maybe up here. (Points to her forehead.)

FRIEDA

And that's where it was, if you ask me. He wasn't on the run from anyone. It's just the sort of tale he would have invented to get his feet under our table.

TRUDI

That isn't true.

FRIEDA

What would you know about it?

TRUDI

He talked to us, Stephen and me. He was scared about something, something in America. He told us he had to leave there in a hurry.

FRIEDA

Which of course you believed.

TRUDI

Yes, I did. You could see he was scared when he talked about it. And I believe it the more now, when it turns out he was here with a forged passport.

GENTLY

So his trouble originated in America . . . wasn't police-trouble . . . was likely to follow him, even here.

FRIEDA

And I say it's all nonsense: and I think I talked to him as much as anyone.

GENTLY

So?

FRIEDA

What do you mean?

GENTLY

You have an alternative explanation – of why your father came here in these circumstances, and was first tortured, then killed?

FRIEDA

What makes you think—

GENTLY

Go on, Miss Frieda.

FRIEDA

No. You can do your own thinking.

GENTLY

I certainly will. Weren't you going to say, What makes me think your father was *murdered*?

FRIEDA

(Paling again.)

If you say so. But—

GENTLY

It's a perfectly good theory. The person who tortured Martin Breske had no good reason to want him dead. Also, the circumstances of the death appear to rule out deliberate homicide. My investigations tell me this. What I'm wondering is, who told you?

FRIEDA

Nobody told me!

GENTLY

A good guess?

FRIEDA

I – yes, I was guessing!

GENTLY

Why guess about that?

FRIEDA

Naturally—

GENTLY

Have we suggested we weren't certain?

FRIEDA

I only thought—

GENTLY

You only thought what I needed investigation to decide. Perhaps you are psychic, Miss Frieda. Or perhaps *you* are not being entirely frank.

FRIEDA

Yes, I tell you—!

GENTLY

Tell me this. Did you trust your father not to talk?

FRIEDA

He swore he wouldn't!

GENTLY

But did you trust him – a weak-willed character like that? Or, in your natural determination to keep the hotel at all costs, didn't you decide on certain steps to make sure this wastrel wouldn't talk?

FRIEDA
(Paler still.)

Never.

GENTLY

This sponger, this parasite.

FRIEDA

No!

GENTLY

This rat in your stores – who deserved no better than poison?

FRIEDA
(Rocking.)

I won't answer you – I won't be talked to like this.

GENTLY

Then let us go back to the previous question. Who told you your father's death was an accident?

No – nobody – it was a guess—

And what information was that man after?

Frieda makes some swerving movements, but still holds on for a few seconds. Her eyes are glazed, her bloodless lips pluck and gibber over her teeth. Then her eyes roll, she lists, she snores, her teeth snap shut with an audible click, and Frieda, Miss Breske, the cloud of thunder, goes lumping down in a dead faint. See to her, Gently says to Sally Dicks, but Trudi is already beside her cousin. Between them they hoist Miss Breske on the sofa and pack two cushions beneath her feet. Mrs Breske makes no movement, no gesture, sits gooseberry-eyed and oscillating. Trudi fetches brandy from chunky decanter, but knows not exactly how to administer it. Miss Breske moans, moves her head from side to side. Drink this, drink this, Frieda, Trudi says. She tips the glass to her cousin's lips and her cousin moves her head and spills it. Then her eyes flicker open, fall on Trudi, the brandy. She makes a weak-strong movement, like a newly born calf: pushes the brandy, Trudi, from her, shudders, turns her face into the sofa.

GENTLY

Miss Breske . . . can you hear what I'm saying?

MRS BRESKE

Ach, leave her alone, leave her alone!

I have no more questions at present. But I must repeat a warning I gave your daughter.

MRS BRESKE

Poor Frieda, poor Frieda. Ach, is the way of all Polizei. In every place, in every country, so it is with these Menschen.

GENTLY

Miss Breske, listen carefully. It is plain your father had a valuable secret. I don't think the torturer got it from him, but your father may well have passed it on to you. If you know, then you may be in danger, because the people who want it are powerful and ruthless; also, you are running that risk unnecessarily, since we shall certainly learn the secret in the end. You have nothing to gain by keeping quiet.

FRIEDA

Go away from me. Go away.

GENTLY

Do you understand? You cannot profit by it.

FRIEDA
(Whispers.)

Go away.

CHAPTER TEN

G ENTLY IS JOVIAL. He walks out of the parlour, where nothing and nobody is faintly jocund, smiling, or rather issuing smiles, and with the step of a man closing shop for the day. His smiles are peculiar. They seem to bubble up like the freshets of a stream in his humoursome eyes, and to play about his mouth, which pipe-free is wicked, with a thousand sunny, comic slants. You cannot nail him down to one smile. His smiling is Protean, first and last. From the merest glimmer and shadow of smile it proceeds, ever-changing, to silent laughter, a magnificent sunburst of unsuppressible delight. So that's that, he smiles at Shelton, towing the local man down the hall. Nothing yet, he smiles at the newshawks, who leap up attentively from their gambling. But that smile lies, as Shelton knows, for Gently is stuffed with news-able matter, and a shame it will be if the nation's breakfast-table is deprived of this rare intelligence. But nothing yet, the smile goes, one of that tremendous armoury, and the newshawks sink back to their cards and little piles and heaps of money. Could Shelton have smiled them off?

Not he: they'd have been at his throat in a trice. But Shelton is not a smiling man: can grin a little, has no smile.

So that's that, Gently repeats, in the garden, still towing Shelton. Now all that remains is to watch and wait for that information from America. We cannot quite yet pull in our suspect because this link in the chain remains open and while it is open our suspect is suspect because one other suspect is also available. But the way is cleared, we are over the hill, another day, at most, should see us home. I could have put more pressure on Frieda Breske, but to save a few hours, it was not necessary. And he flicks skywards, a twirling saucer, the white-bladed head of a marguerite, which he has plucked in pure wantonness and now as wantonly casts away. But, frowning Shelton says, at what point did you guess Clooney's identity? From the first, Gently says, who was more likely than the lady's husband to be domiciled here? So when his accent changed – His accent? At first, it was native Bronx, Gently explains, then it became tinctured with European and at last settled towards Germany – this, together with his otherwise inexplicable choice of retreats, and the various attitudes towards him of the Breskes, strongly suggested who he was. Then finally Klapper, who you ably interrogated. His contribution was critical. For who would attract to himself such a nickname as Heifetz, unless, like Martin Breske, he was a fiddler? Heifetz applies to no other distinction, no racial, physical characteristic. Our intelligence from America gave confirmation. It was child's-play then to pump the Breskes. Yes, child's-play, Shelton agrees, and really believes it at that moment, with a picture of the obdurate Frieda beaten to the ground still fresh, still wondrous, in his eye.

Gently casts another marguerite, giving this one a downward-skimming flight. Also from the first, he says, one thing bearing on another, I was looking for some family skeleton which Clooney could rattle. If indeed he were a stranger it were very strange that he could establish himself as an unpaying guest, yet if he were Breske was it less strange, unless he, Breske, had dangerous knowledge? How dangerous? What affecting? Immediately one thought of that inheritance. Then of Trudi, so unlike her sister, and of the photograph, so like Trudi. An interplay of genes? Yes, arguable; but how much simpler if Trudi were a Lindemann! And Mitzi Lindemann died, I was informed, at just that time when the Breskes fled. If all this were so, if Breske knew it, his wife and daughter were under his thumb; by opening his mouth he could bring tumbling hotel, prosperity, about their ears. Which Miss Frieda wouldn't take lying down, Shelton says. But which, in its way, helps our understanding not much, Gently says. But Miss Frieda – Tush, Gently says (and he is a man who can say it with authority), however you set it up he was her father and for her to kill him would be parricide. There are parricides, but they are rare, and extremely rare when premeditated. I have never at any time been disposed to regard Miss Frieda as the killer. She, Shelton gasps, had opportunity! She couldn't prove where she was all the time. Oh, Gently says, and oh! Can you imagine her overpowering her father? Shelton swallows and stares at a rosebed. Perhaps he can imagine such a feat of Miss Frieda. Gently downed her, but Gently aside, Shelton has a high respect for Frieda, Miss Breske.

No, Gently says, the situation was unfortunate, but it could scarcely have led to what followed, unless you suppose that somebody tortured Breske to learn what hold he had on his family. But such a supposition is unproductive. It takes no notice of why Breske came to England. We have to understand why he vanished in New York and reappeared here with a false passport. He needed no desperate measures of this kind to come on a sponging trip to his family, and if he told his wife the truth, he was not in trouble with the police. Then with whom? Gently plucks a marguerite and, Buddha-like, raises it for Shelton's enlightenment; but Shelton remains this side of beyond and greets the act with no comprehending smile. Yet the answer is simple. We don't know, Gently says. We are hoping the New York police can tell us. Though, and this is purely a hunch, I shall not be surprised to learn it has to do with Pat, Toni and Abdul. With a criminal organization! Shelton flashes. Certainly that, Gently says. Perhaps, Shelton says, staring at the marguerite – which may yet put his feet in the way – an organization connected with the Nazis, with some big Nazi, as big as Eichmann. Perhaps, Gently says, also regarding the flower, though the names do not sound persuasively Aryan. But in their present state of adversity the ex-Nazi Party leaders may not be too rigorously doctrinaire. It could be Bormann, Shelton breathes, I read a book about him, nobody knows for sure he's dead. He could be hiding in New York as well as anywhere else. Don't they have a Nazi Party there? So I understand, Gently says. And what a spot it would be for him, Shelton enlarges, right at the centre, where he can play his games, make a new bid for world power. And it makes sense. Look what's been happening. A liberal president popped off. Race riots tearing the country apart, the Ku Klux Klan, the Black Moslems. And General Motors alienated, Gently says, but that's taking us rather far afield. I don't know, Shelton says, about General Motors, but the rest of it reads like Nazi strategy. And if Breske knew, knew about Bormann – I'd say Bormann was the most likely – that would account for him skipping, all right, and the false passport and everything. Which would give us a pointer, Gently says. Shelton nods eagerly. Israeli patriots! Have we many of them around? Gently inquires. Shelton glares at the flower. But his mind is buzzing.

They stroll further. Gently retains the flower, which now somehow symbolizes the discussion, is a badge, a warning to all comers that the lairds are at their cracks. Shelton has it in his eye. Gently ponders it, daps the air with it. There is faint scent from the broken stalk, from the button of trumpets, scent. The scent is sweetish, sharpish, autumnal, though autumn is nowhere in the sky, not in the seasound, not in the witch-oak beneath which Trudi and Stephen sprawled. Yet autumn is somewhere about that spot, to evoke so strongly in the marguerite's scent. It may be that dying Breske sent the season on before. You meant what you told them, Shelton broods, about his death being an accident? Can you, Gently replies, interpret what happened in any other light? Breske escaped from his torturer, but in escaping ran over the cliff. By chance he ran over above the pill-box. No theory of intent can explain the circumstance. Neither can it: and Shelton once more feels the bruising weight of a superior vessel. For had not he himself, though without actually achieving it, come to the brink of this conclusion? He had worked for suicide, so hard! He had argued to it and at last beyond it. Then, left with murder, he had teased and wrestled the facts to understand how murder could be. And he'd reached the brink: had found he could explain neither of these 'theories of intent' – but left it there. Gently, at that point, had turned his back and walked on. Sad Shelton! He is not used to making these existentialist leaps, is at once alarmed, indignant, and cast down. How dare Gently proceed like this? Shelton seeks a loop-hole. It could still have been suicide! Only hitting the box need be accidental. Gently raises the flower, says, Occam's Razor, and smiles. Occam's Razor? Shelton is ignorant of this celebrated shaver, but he gathers the general tone of the smile, realizes Gently, in some way, has him.

What follows from it, Gently says, sniffing the button of the marguerite (and thus further irritating Shelton, who begins vaguely to feel the flower is his enemy), is that Breske was chased, and hence had so far not revealed his information, because if he had revealed it the torturer would have done with him and he need not have been in such a panic. We assume here that the information relates to a criminal matter, which Breske could not reveal to the police, to whom thus he would not dare complain. A criminal matter, frowns Shelton. You mean, Breske himself is a wanted Nazi? The precise category of the criminal matter we wait to hear, Gently says. It is considerable, we know this, or Breske wouldn't have skipped to England, nor would he have been pursued to such a distance, or be expecting such pursuit. The gentlemen who ate with Breske in Cassidy's Restaurant, if they appear in this affair, do not seem by themselves a force adequate to mount a transatlantic manhunt. I expect to hear of an organization. The Nazis, Shelton says, everything points to it. An organization, Gently says, with, to put it no higher, international associates. It may be political, may be criminal, not unlikely is both, but however, is large. Breske was doubtful if he could hide from it. What a hell of a position, Shelton says, my God, to know they are coming for you. Not to be able to run anywhere where they won't get you at last. Yes, Gently agrees, a hell of a position. It is living a posthumous existence. You died when the hunt was up but had no benefit of not being. I wouldn't, Shelton says, have been in his shoes for all the tea in China. Yet it is just our position, Gently says, except his was short term, ours is long. Life's Razor. Shelton stares. But damn it, he says, we can live with *that*. Perhaps he, too, could live with his, Gently says. And perhaps after all it is no evil.

Shelton is silent, thinking of Breske, the body, X, (X) Clooney, sometime Stenke, the man, once a youth, once a boy, once a child: unimaginably cradled in that unimaginable city, amorphously known to Shelton, for the most part, as a name encountered in coach-tour literature, though not that either, entirely, since buried now by fretting time. What strange and tortuous ways brought little Martin to his dark tower? How many journeys, short and long, had he taken to reach that goal? Already his small feet tapping the pavement by the bright Rosenkavalier poster were trotting, trotting through

175

Hapsburg Wien towards the concrete nugget, then unenvisaged. And the faltering bow, slowly mastered, squeaked and droned of his coming, and ten thousand phrases lodged in his brain to marshal him the road he went: and the eager kisses of Edith Tichtel, one more being one less, and the new sorrow of wrinkled Frieda, drove him on, on, on. Wars hurried his step, shrill revolution, women, smile melting in smile, streets, houses, stairs, beds, the thickening face his brush lathered: seasons, ever less-prosperous, hopes, never hugged home, pleasures, barely mantling boredom, sorrows, each with double-sting – march, Breske, march! Change the Old World for the New! Set your back to that lump of concrete and march on: till you meet it. Because you know, Martin Breske, you must hit that bugger head-on, and not the stars staying in their courses, not prayer like thunder, can alter that. The midwife's slap sent you wauling to your brief pilgrimage, here. But why, why? Shelton asks, wide-eyed, fronting unreason with his indignation. Why not, Shelton? What's in question? Doesn't a man live till he dies?

No, I wouldn't have been him, Shelton shivers. What that poor bastard must have gone through. You should have seen his face. I'd have talked if someone worked me over like that. Perhaps he did, Gently shrugs, but that's not my reading of the matter. His torturer could not conveniently be his executioner, though probably Breske was marked for killing. Somewhere else, more anonymously, shot, perhaps, from a passing car, would have been the end of Martin Breske, if he had talked, and not died as he did. We were not to be interested, yet.

Breske killing himself was unfortunate. Because he did we have stepped in prematurely to the possible prejudice of someone important. So I read it. Then you know, Shelton says, you know the identity of the torturer. Why yes, Gently says, I can hazard a guess on the strength of your interrogations today. His interrogations! Shelton is dumbfounded, would wither the marguerite with his glare. In all that sweaty, grinding routine, where did he uncover a pearl of this price? But Gently says he has, and Gently is honourable, says not what he cannot make good: will make good, sans doubt, when next the American oracle speaks. Dare Shelton guess too? He casts about wildly, but cannot make his suspicion take root. And cruel Gently only raises his flower, against the blue sea, the bluer sea-sky.

CHAPTER ELEVEN

NIGHT AGAIN.

Shelton has gone, with his frowns and frustrations, setting inland the English grille of his English Oxford Mark 6; with him also, by his side, Walters, who knows well when to button his lip, and in the back Sally Dicks, nursing a fat folder of scribble. Gone, and silently gone: no comment passed during the journey: Shelton, Walters and Sally, dumbly proceeding in the Oxford: till twenty miles on they reach headquarters, home, the place where Shelton is Somebody, the hub of a world in his size and which, in his fashion, he knows to control. There somebody will say to him (in fact it is the duty sergeant, Godbold, who says it), What was he like, sir, the Big Fellow? Did you get on with him all right? And Shelton will thaw enough to admit, You can always talk to these big blokes, adding, You can sometimes learn a thing or two from them. It's good to work with them now and then.

Night again!

Stody too has driven away in his modest heap, and even the newshawks, dined on a statement, have drawn off all their force but two. These two, having no beds, play a wicked game of brag in the hall lounge, till midnight breaks up the school and they seek a drowse on the settles. Gently, they know, sleeps above them – and tomorrow the world shall know it too; because he, the beloved of all their tribe, has laid his head on the dead man's pillow; while (X) Clooney cools still in the mortuary, he, the Man, the avenger, warms (X) Clooney's sheets: blankets, at all events: and of such stuff are captions made. And sleep he may: for has it not, somehow (and nobody quite knows how, whether Shelton was indiscreet, or Gently himself, in talking to the reporters, could not quite conceal it), got about that one more phone call will do the Great Man's business for him, and that for this, this only he waits, before dropping his hand on the guilty shoulder? Indeed that message went into the grapevine. The strained, scared Breskes had obviously heard it. It flew round the guests, who all had it at dinner, and perhaps from them to the waiters and the kitchen quarters. The musicians knew it: they discussed it between numbers, played it as false notes in Lehar and Offenbach; Trudi knew it; Stephen Halliday knew it; it may even have reached the village via Stody and Brother Fred. So Gently may sleep, whoever else doesn't, in that gone-to-bed building by the sea, though lying in the room, on the very mattress, of him who now sleeps to wake no more. Breske's avenger, surely, is secure from Breske's ghost.

Night again . . .

Southwards the lights of the resort town wink out, gemmed lacework, visible from the cliff, the attic dormers of the hotel, winking suddenly, leaving black, though still supporting a glowing gloom, the stooping, heavy, promontorial outward swing of the coast. And a moon shows, a sickle moon, soon to charm up the herring. It stitches goldeny the scaly sea below the dewed furzes of the cliff. Where Clooney (he was Clooney then) went the hunting natterjacks run, but cannot see, as he could not, the moondull concrete under the cliff. Will his ghost walk here? Brother Fred doesn't see it, nor does skinny Sid Balls, as they run their boat down the beach. The boat goes soft and even into the wash which is little more than a lakeshore fret, rocks them aboard, is poled out, rowed away, its one lamp swaying. And Brother Fred, if he thinks of Clooney (for Brother Fred is facing shorewards as he dips, hauls, dips, hauls, his arms of oak fresh and free), does so confusedly, his only image of him being of a chill corpse, not a man; So Am Not I, tending to be the line of thought of Brother Fred. And the lamp sways paler and the oars thud lighter and the boat grows dimmer in the dark sea, and at last a faint firefly, coming and going, is all a shore watcher may see of the fishermen. Sea-silence then, which is silence enough. A lisp and babble at the world's edge. On the cliff, the lightest rustle as a natterjack darts, pounces. A manner of coolness or breathing in the air which has no direction, is not a breeze, will not stir or set murmuring the least filament of grass or ling. On such a night may not he walk, the man who here violently ended, and his squareset mouth again rupture the dim dome of heaven?

Night, the darker hours.

Overmuch sleep at the Hotel Continental. One light

only, that in the hall, where the two reporters hunch on their settles. The doors are bolted, the Aquarium locked. The big stairs have never a creak in them. The shadowy landing, the long corridors, have slippered silence built in. House silence: the silence of sleepers, arrested, contained by walls, bars: silence not quite silent, yet the listener hears no sound. Is there a listener? A reporter stirs, moans discontent, blinks at his watch; moans again and burrows at the settle: only its hardness has waked him. The other reporter, also uneasy, twists his head in the search for comfort, and by doing so provokes a choking snore, which spurs him to twist his head again. Overmuch sleep! But who should be waking in this building's many mansions, in the deep shadow between sun and sun, before Brother Fred has shot his nets? Lovers have finished with their loving, talkers have had their talk out, worriers have worried themselves to slumber, there are none sick, in pain. Yet . . . overmuch sleep! Though that bell is not now ringing, though dead Breske stays dead, does not walk, and no thief stands by the window. Across at the village (and autumn is in it, as it was in the smell of the marguerite: a frost in the sound, frozen moonlight) hysterically laughs a little owl, and again, and again: the humour of some droll slaughter: and none to hear him, here or there, or cast a thought to his jolly murder. Or do the sleepers turn at the sound? In their dark oceans, does it start a dream? Is it this or some other that begins to beat and beat in their ear like muffled drum? Do they truly dream, or wake, hearing this sound far away, thumping, thumping, with behind it, more remote still, sleep-murdering . . . screams? Overmuch sleep! But sleep's away, if not the dream, suddenly exploding. Doors slam, lights flash, and the screams go on, peal by peal. Shapes, rushing down the dim corridors, shapes, pounding up the stairs, calling, shouting, shrieks of women, and the screams, and the screams. Who is it screaming? Down by the landing, where is no light except from the hall, is the shape that screams, in the fecund shadows, pale, with a glistening darkness at her bosom. And the darkness spreads as she screams and the darkness spots on the carpet and on the wall which she hugs is the darkness, dripping, rolling in fat streaks. Lights, oh lights! Here's bloody Frieda, tolling the skies with her throbbing throat, bleeding her life over her lap, sliding, gurgling down the wall. She's stabbed, stabbed, and her screams go out, she crumples, sprawls, moans, bleeds: lays her head against the wall, shuddering, groaning through her teeth. Oh lights! They find the switch. Merciful God, the blood, the blood! What will stop it? Who can staunch it? How keep that little life from flowing out?

And comes the Man.

With never a word he takes the bloody girl in his arms, strides to her room, from which blood trails, and lays her on her dishevelled bed. He rips her bloody nightdress from her and wads it in a pad for her bloody breast, then jams it into the rippling wound and bears upon it, calling for bandages. Frieda's white face turns and turns, her eyes roll. Who? he whispers. She doesn't hear him, moans, turns, gives a shivering sigh and faints away. Bandages come: he lashes the pad, the oozing pad, tight to her breast. One of you keep pressure on it, he orders, and three step forward to be that one. Chiefie, I've rung the doctor, pants a reporter, he's fetching an ambulance from town. Shall I ring your people? Yes, Gently says, tell them to get out right away. But he himself is standing still, staring about the meagre room, eyes, no longer mild, thrusting, stripping, eating up minute detail. The window is open top and bottom. He strides to it, stares out. Trudi comes flying in at that moment, falls on her knees, sobbing, at the bedside. Where is Mrs Breske, Trudi? God knows! Frieda – oh, Frieda! He is out of the room. Who has seen Mrs Breske? Nobody: nobody has seen that lady. He breaks through the crowd, begins to run, races down the long corridor, the corridor still reaching into shadow, and thunderously pounds on the Breskeian door. Mrs Breske! She must hear him! Nobody living can be so deaf! He crashes the door in – to find Mrs Breske sleeping, snoring, in a four-poster bed. Wake up, wake up, Mrs Breske! But no, she slumbers raucously on. He shakes her – still the snores come. Will anyone wake that woman again? He switches on the light. The rococo room, stuffed with treasures of old Vienna, with a certain scent of stale lavender, and a furtiveness, spreads about him. Here too the window is open. He doesn't go to this window. On the lower frame of the window he can see, quite clearly, the marks of three bloody fingers. He glances at the door, where the guests are crowding, at the bed, where snores the unconscious woman; then, moving silently, he approaches the bed, and, with a great heave, sends it rolling.

What happens then? There are seven witnesses with a clear view through the door, and likely, if their testimony is taken, they will scarcely agree on two points. Certainly,

183

Gently's body is between them and whatever the bed conceals, and certainly, his act of heaving the bed, and the sight of it rolling, may surprise and divert their gaze for a moment. Yet still there are seven, with fourteen eyes, and a well-lit scene acting before them, and they, moreover, in a degree prepared for what may and does transpire when the bed is rolled. A snarl, or cry: can they agree to that? No! Three of the seven never heard it, one describes it as a shriek, one an oath, another a groan. The knife, then? One, one only – and he saw little else beside – can fix the knife, and fix it for ever, hovering in air, like Macbeth's dagger. A kitchen knife, about a foot long – he can almost read the cutler's name for you – with a black handle, bloodied, occupying a space nor'west of the lampshade. Who saw the hand with the knife struck up? Not a soul of the seven. The karate sweep which changed to a fist-blow? Yes, it was nailed in one pair of eyes. They saw the hand raised, flat, chopper-like, saw it flash on its deadly journey, saw, suddenly, the hand ball to a fist, divert from throat to a stockinged jaw. A hammering blow! The jaw jerked aside from it, then was jerked back by a hook as crushing. All done in a never-to-be-forgotten split second: murder: murder with one hand. And the man with the knife, though none saw him with it? If the door had been closed on those early impressions? Alas for the testimony of mortals! – but two of the seven had seen him single. Four, would have been the guess of the witness who could report the knife in such accurate image, and counting heads must have yielded, two, while a vociferous three would have mocked the poll. As well these impressions could be corrected, unlike many that

184

come to court! Four, three, two inchoate assailants are chopped as one to the bedroom floor. And now they see (and may at last agree, though agreement may hold no longer than seeing) he is dressed in black, in a black track-suit, with a lady's black stocking pulled over his head. He is dazed, but not senseless. Get up, Gently commands: Gently mighty in a fawn dressing-gown (point unimportant, yet which will be remembered with the hovering knives and oath/groans) – Get up. And the man claws to his knees: wobbles: holds out his hand: says hoarsely, Don't, don't hit me again. I won't do anything, I promise. Don't hit me. Take that thing off, Gently says. The man, who is shaking, can scarcely do this. He tugs hopelessly at the slinking nylon which rides taut over his chin. Then it gives. And so they see him. And thus they may answer, if called to witness, being asked: Do you see that man in court? – pointing to the dock, Yes: Carlo Gordini.

Carlo Gordini! For there he kneels, a mulberry bruise on his handsome jaw, his black eyes wide, expecting blows, on his hands, in his finger crooks, Frieda Breske's blood. Handsome Carlo, gentle Carlo. Whose mistress has snored through all this commotion, and who slumbers on, may slumber ever, but dream no more of lost Vienna. And Gently says to him: I was bluffing you, Carlo. Your name wasn't coming to me from America. You should have sat tight, Carlo. I knew you did it, but I couldn't tie you in yet. But now you're for it, Carlo, and that's double trouble, puts you in the same boat as Martin Breske. So you'd better help us by coming clean, because at least, with us, you'll stay alive. What did you give her? Carlo swallows, gazes, perhaps, you think, hasn't heard Gently, but then says, very low and husky, Just aspirins. Ten. To make her sleep. And the same the last time? Maybe not so many. Tonight I want her sleeping sound. While you tortured, then murdered, her daughter? – No, don't answer that, Gently says.

And still night . . .

Brother Fred, with longshores flapping around his boots, catching silverily the hurricane's yellow, sees the hotel lit up like a lighthouse. Vehicle lights sweep round and to it, each pair flashing out to sea: he counts two, three, four, but may have missed one while shaking loose the herring. Something up, he says to skinny Sid, blast, don't say that bugger is at it again. I wouldn't put it past him, says skinny Sid. They get a taste for it, that's what I reckon. Wonder who he's done this time. Brother Fred stops hauling, gazes, phosphorescence dripping from his hooked hands, across the slow sea, whose heaving hillocks splits the far lights in tremulous flakes. Get these bloody nets in, he says, Christ, it could as well be Brother Jim. If that sod has stuck a knife into him – These foreigners'll do anything, skinny Sid says. And they haul and haul, but not yet may come where the starry lights burn their message, and where others are beforehand, including, could they know, hale though unshaven, Brother Jim. Halliday has been, done and gone, bringing, leaving with Trudi, young Stephen. Has she fetched up blood? was Halliday's first question, and, being told, No, he's optimistic. Not a stab, he reports to Gently, but more of a slash, though deep. I have her blood group, which saves time. Don't think we'll have a tragedy here. And Mrs

Breske? Oh, she'll live. She certainly snores as though she may. She snores down the stairs, through the hall, into the ambulance, and goes off snoring beside silent Frieda. Shelton meanwhile has come, with his leal team at his back. Staring at handcuffed Carlo, Shelton endures his bitterest pang of all this case. Because Shelton was there: he'd done his homework: had, near as a toucher, rung Gently: only hadn't, to be able to say to Gently's face, Of course, Gordini is our man, sir. And now, now . . . ! What wretched star is crossing the fate of unhappy Shelton? He had only asked to play second fiddle, just the once, to Gently's first. Stody, who guards Carlo, and asked nothing, knows more felicity than poor Shelton, though Stody, too, has his bitters: Carlo's hands wring Stody's heart.

Night: but a paling out to sea, saying dawn is not far.

I must borrow the parlour again, Gently tells Trudi, who is sobbing quietly in Stephen's arms. Into the parlour then go Carlo's hands, Stody one pace behind, hands together, steel-linked, swelled, clenched, knuckle to knuckle. Sit there. The hands sit. The hands, like a stump, thrusting out before. Carlo, his black curls sweat-limp, hunches over the hands, may not turn from them his face. You guard the door, please, Gently says to Stody, and Stody goes gratefully to that station. Prepare to take a statement, Gently says to Sally Dicks, in case Gordini chooses to make one. Sally prepares. Gently sits before Carlo. Between them the hands go tight, pull apart. The black track-suit is shadow, head, face are both shadow; alone, not shadow, the trumpet hands. Gordini, Gently says. Carlo says nothing. Gordini, listen to me carefully.

You are not obliged to say anything at this time, but if you do, it will be taken down in writing, may be used in evidence. Do you understand what I'm saying? The hands lift, Carlo nods. I want you to answer me in words, Gently says. Yes, Carlo says. Sally writes.

GENTLY

Now perhaps you'd like to tell me, Gordini, what you were doing on Tuesday night.

CARLO

I didn't kill him!

GENTLY

Never mind that.

CARLO

But you gotta believe me about this! It was all a balls-up, they didn't want him killed, they were going to take care of him after I'd left. Man, they use pros when they want to knock them off, not Johnny-on-the-spot. Ain't that sense?

GENTLY

Your mission was limited to making him talk.

CARLO

Yeah, yeah, and I wasn't to mark him where it showed. They didn't want nobody poking their nose in before the stuff was out of the country. But the sonofabitch just kept on squealing, I couldn't get him to open up. And he was a strong bastard. He kneed me plenty. I'm still sore where that bastard kneed me.

188

GENTLY

He escaped you.

CARLO

Isn't that what I'm saying?

GENTLY

You chased him.

CARLO

Sure. He still hadn't talked.

GENTLY

Over the cliff.

CARLO

Man, could I help it which way the sonofabitch ran?

GENTLY

But you didn't try to stop him, I suppose, Gordini?
Like shouting to him he was heading for the edge?

CARLO

Sure, I would have done if I'd thought, but I didn't,
did I? It happened too quick. He nearly creased me
putting his knee in, he knew I'd cut him some more for
that, and man, he just took off like a rabbit and went
straight over. How could I help it?

GENTLY

An accidental death.

CARLO

Yeah, accidental. You gotta see that. I didn't kill him.
They didn't want it that way, I was treating him soft,
he'd've behaved like normal the next morning.

GENTLY

And just now was an accident?

CARLO

Sure it was an accident, I'd never have cut that bitch at all. You got me wrong, mister, I'm no killer. I didn't go in there to cut her.

And his sweating face, the brows so loaded that he must frown not to spill their burden, turns up to Gently's, glistening, still handsome, though marred by a bruise and the insolent eyes.

GENTLY

What made you suppose Miss Breske could help you?

CARLO

She had a better chance, she'd know where to look.

GENTLY

She knew what you were after?

CARLO

She caught me, the bitch, I had to tell her what it was about.

GENTLY

Caught you when?

CARLO

Tuesday night. She must have been watching from her window. She saw me climbing into the old girl's room. I had to tell her or she'd've talked.

GENTLY

So she knew you were the man.

CARLO

Sure, she knew about everything. I was all shook up with Clooney and that or I might've figured an angle. But man, she wasn't going to talk, not with all that dough lying around, and I reckoned if she found it first I could soon take it off her.

GENTLY

How much was it?

CARLO

Two hundred grand. They busted a bank vault some place.

GENTLY

They were sure he brought it here with him?

CARLO

Yeah. He didn't stop running till he got here. They had a private dick pick him up soon as he set foot in this country. They're big, man, big. You don't cross them up and get away with it.

GENTLY

I imagine they don't like incompetence, either.

CARLO

(With a quick glance round.)
But you promised—

GENTLY

Don't worry. You'll be very well protected for longer than Cosa Nostra will bother about you. You were only on probation, after all.

CARLO

It's a lie! When I got to the States—

GENTLY

You were promised big things, no doubt. But I imagine Montelli was only using you.

Carlo shakes the sweat from his eyes and glares up at the Great Man, who knows everything, and who perhaps has just voiced a secret fear of Carlo's own. But the Great Man has no expression, where he sits, fronting Carlo, so large, so heavy, so monumental, allowing Carlo to destroy himself.

GENTLY

When did he brief you for this job?

CARLO
(Sulkily.)

It doesn't matter.

GENTLY

He would scarcely waste money calling you direct—

CARLO

As though that worried him! Giovanni!

GENTLY

Then we can trace the call.

CARLO

It was last month – why should I remember when? And again on Saturday—

Yes, of course. Your cousin was wondering if he could trust you.

CARLO

(Stares at Gently, strains at the handcuffs.)

GENTLY

With such a sum involved, it was natural. Once you got your hands on that you might well be tempted to double-cross him. Montelli gave you the job, he was answerable for you, he had pressure on him from higher up. When you didn't show results he'd get worried, maybe start using threats.

CARLO

It wasn't that way!

GENTLY

He didn't threaten you?

CARLO

Sure, all right, he was acting heavy! But that don't mean he didn't trust me, he knew I'd come through in the end.

GENTLY

But he was getting worried.

CARLO

So he was. Maybe I hadn't played it right. Maybe I should've got rough with Clooney sooner, not poked around looking for the dough. I hadn't never done a job before, I didn't figure the right way to do it, so he was getting worried, all right. That ain't the same as not trusting.

GENTLY

Did he tell you to use the knife?

CARLO

Yeah, maybe. To cut him a little.

GENTLY

In the stomach.

CARLO

Ain't that sense? It gets them scared, and it don't show.

GENTLY

And you intended to treat Miss Breske the same?

CARLO

Sure, I wasn't going to cut her bad. But the stupid bitch goes blowing her top and horsing around. I couldn't help it.

GENTLY

You seem to have been unfortunate, Carlo.

CARLO

Yeah, unfortunate. I missed the breaks. But don't never say Giovanni couldn't trust me, mister, because that ain't so. I just missed out.

GENTLY

Tell me one thing, Gordini.

CARLO

Sure, sure.

Was Clooney dead when you left him down there?

Man, I just took off, I didn't inquire. He was trouble enough. Ain't that sense?

Sense enough, it would appear, since Gently asks no more questions, lets Carlo make his point, all his points, to persuade, if they will, a jury yet uncalled. And Carlo sits back, feeling maybe he's scored, maybe he's put up a good front, need sweat a little less now he's explained so well what, in the first place, was merely bad luck.

I'd best get a search-warrant, Shelton says to Gently, when the latter rises, goes towards the door. If that money is here we'll have to find it, though it means tearing the place down. Do you reckon it's still here? Gently shrugs, Why not? Gordini certainly hasn't found it, and if Frieda did, then she either left it where it was, or re-hid it, on the premises. Where would Shelton have hidden it? Shelton looks blank, says, In a cistern, chimney, that sort of place. – Where searchers, of course, would look for it, Gently says, but where, to our best knowledge, they didn't find it. Well, then, in the roof, Shelton says, under the floorboards, in books, a mattress, the top of a wardrobe; in an outhouse maybe, or in the cellar, in a flour-bin, fridge, lampshade, switchbox. Yet Gordini searched for a month, Gently says, in such places, and lately Frieda, with better knowledge. So they missed it, Shelton says, but it has to be there. Nobody thought of a new place yet. I wonder, Gently says. He goes out into the hall, where reporters swarm like September wasps, and where Trudi, last left representative of the Breskes, though tearful, maintains her ground and authority. Miss Trudi, Gently says, if you had money, notes, to hide, where a good searcher wouldn't find them, in this hotel, where would you put it? Money, Trudi says wondering, a lot of money? A fair bulk of it, Gently says. Not enough to fill that carved chest, but still plenty. Say a hatbox full. Trudi stares about the hall, not hopeful, not thinking an answer seriously intended, till, her eye reaching the alpenhorn above the Aquarium, she says, carelessly, I'd stick it in that! Have it down, Gently says to Stody, and Stody, with a chair, performs the feat: nine perilous feet of monster horn come wavering down from their high station. See what's in it! Stody pokes a moment, draws a wad of newspaper from the trumpet mouth: peers: gets the alpenhorn on his shoulder: braces himself: heaves, tilts. And there it is, and out it comes: money, money, with more money: a sliding stream of banded rolls, to scatter and heap on the hall tiles.

O man of fortune! Even this last flourish has come to hand in your triumph, picked from the air like a conjurer's silk, a wanton gesture to applause. And the reporters, adoring as they may their idol, their never-failing fountain of copy, surround him, where he stands, with staggering Stody, to burn flash-bulbs without end. Haydon, thou shouldst be living yet to masterpaint this ranging scene! See how they group to the marvellous focus of Triumph and The New Cornucopia! And above them, ascending to the landing's gloom, the admiring guests in night attires, with, aside, such studies as Shelton,

196

the star-crossed man; Trudi, beauty in amaze; and shackled Carlo, the bloody-handed, whose eyes would unhinge all creation. More, while this holds, open flies the door, admitting the ocean-planing light of dawn, and anxiety, presented by Brother Fred, with augury, skinny Sid Balls; while the lover, Stephen, the worshipper, Sally, and caution, Walters, in their several postings, add, continue, enrich all ways the diverse and epic composition. Seize it, some Haydon of later day! It is worth another ten-year labour. The camera lies: there is no truth but as it is felt and given to feel.

CHAPTER TWELVE

A cool sea and a cool sky are the mode of Friday morning, grey above grey, both pale, and still, soft-going as a seaside may be.

What news, where all has been news? There is no Breske to preside at breakfast. Trudi is encamped at the County Hospital, will scarcely be seen again all day. Notwithstanding, the coffee comes hot and breakfast goes its common gait, for the hour has found its man: plump Rudi Dorfmann, who has the Breske touch, and joys to apply it. All is the same, though all is changed, is the note at the Hotel Continental. Nothing, under Rudi, may be expected, in the way of slack service, to hint at sensation the night before. So they must concede (heavy-eyed breakfasters) that dull routine is again in threat, and that soon, barring tennis, putting or flirting, no large excitements will remain to try. Certainly some early ones (most were late) witnessed sponging operations on the landing; indeed, the papers are lurid, with promise of more and better to come; but the thing's self, the action, is complete, may lead no further; is subject for rounding and analysis only, has stopped as short as B.C. Lost, except in its effects, which to the guests are a secondary concern: as, how Mrs Breske recovered from snoring, was quickly her mournful, querulous self; how Frieda fared, how long on blood, on saline drip: when conscious; with what indignation Gordini heard himself, after all, charged with murder. Lost, and yielding a sense of loss; in sensation's ruins the guests sit; they have been too spoiled and gorged with excitements to find a gust for the cold meats now. When Carlo went, all went that was mainspring to the action. Gently himself, without Carlo, begins sinking towards moderate humanity.

So the tide is ebbing, ebbing, ebbing, when at last the bells tolls, when Cyrus Fleischer, full of bubble, pours out his budget of information; and That Man, sensation's antonym, whose bait of questions caught these answers, is seen, for he takes the call in the Aquarium, to look almost bored as flesh is given to the bones he knew. Yes, for sure, Breske, or Stenke, has been linked to the three men, Pat, Toni and Abdul, now identified as Patrick O'Malley, Toni Guzzi and Benjamin Stephanopoulos; and sure, more sure, they are professional criminals, enjoying the protection of the local gang-boss, one Montelli, a Sicilian by birth, and connected up to his ears. And, says Fleischer, though proof is to seek, these men pulled a job on the night of 10 May, inasmuch as they curiously entered, by precise excavation, the strongroom of a bank in East 56th Street. Curiously entered, because by the ceiling, from the office of some insurance brokers above, a feat requiring very special knowledge of the exact location of the strongroom. How obtained? At first a mystery, but now becoming sharply clear. The building was a project of that same firm by whom Stenke/Breske had been employed. Stenke/Breske could have studied the plans, provided the very special knowledge; in fact, most certainly surely must have done so, and concluded his play by heisting the loot. A notable coup by an amateur! The boyo must have been quite a guy. But you didn't do that to the likes of Montelli and expect to live too long afterwards. And the amount stolen? Gently asks flatly. The amount is the same as Stody poured from the horn. All Breske bought with it was twenty-two cuts and a fast farewell, and that was interest. Then Gently exchanges information, promises other returns, hangs up; sits a while, a dead pipe drooping slack between his teeth. He has here set down the pyramid he carried, and which needs carrying by him no more: the weight's gone. What burden he leaves is such as lesser men may carry.

And the guests who watch (they are many) see some tiredness in the sitting man, as though, oh heresy! – he were just another, lacking his sleep, like themselves: no Atlas but common clay, wistful after a job done: one too heavy to rouse himself for the next task in hand. After all, have they mistaken him? Shelton, arriving then, supplies a contrast. Shelton too is tired, but not so tired as to lack his hard, policeman's edge. Shelton is never less than Shelton, though Gently may abdicate from Gently: Shelton's a power, however modest, wherever Shelton happens to be. Then is Gently, too, a kind of make-believe, an attitude bearing a label? Shrewdly selected by omniscient Whitehall to counter a wrong attitude developed here? A brilliant actor, no more, who can strut his part like an Irving, but who, in his dressing-room, the curtain fallen, becomes a dull dog, a block, a stone? Ah, but the heresy is only of a moment! See him rise, now, to greet Shelton! See the tiredness, wistfulness, fall from him, and the eyes twinkle, the mouth shape! The part's in him, not put on, he has no stage but all the world: the fault's in us if we mistake him, seeking to limit him in a mood. The wizard who came, saw and conquered is the very same who smiles at us now, and who will soon step into his bronze-and-black Sceptre and depart, undiminished, from our gaze. Shelton, we shall have always with us: Gently, once, on a herring moon. He is human, ye guests – rejoice! But he is also himself too.

And go he does, and Shelton goes, and the reporters stay only for lunch, and the guests are left with the very tail-end and tough scrag of the affair. Seeing, not clearly, into what has passed, seeing, scarcely at all, into what shall come, or where will end, if it ever ends, the strange convulsion that happened there. For this was a knot or hurricane in time, to which, from which its elements accelerated. Quickly they came, quickly they went, after slow approach, before slow dispersal. And from whence they came was no origin and whither they went is no end: only tied in this knot are they a moment in pattern. Be shapeless again, elements! See Carlo returned to starve in Sicily, nine years later, to quote a figure, which, understand, is quoting chaos; Trudi, see, she's in Canada, a widow with Stephen's one child, Stephen dying, almost casually, in a crash outside a Toronto hospital; fatter, wheezier, Edith Breske, like a grumpy Pekinese, snores now away the rich incomes of three hotels on the coast;

and daughter Frieda is Breske no more, but thin, shrewish Frau Dorfmann – yet a proper mate, though thin, though shrewish, for prospering Rudi: these two childless. True or untrue? Fact or dreaming? Return to the knot or hurricane! Stay there, with the disconsolate guests, and Gently's smoothly-driven exit. Stody, who interested The Man, got promotion before Christmas, and Shelton, by a retirement, was made happy, or what passed for happy, too.

NORWICH, *July '64–September '66*